CLAIMING DEATH

CHANGER SERIES BOOK 2

A. C. WILDS

CONTENTS

First edition

Editing: Kala Adams

Proofreading: Robin Lee - Rainy Day Editing

Cover Design: Nichole Witholder - Rainy Day Artwork

Formatting: BBB Publishing Services

❈ Created with Vellum

DEADICATION

To my husband - The earth shattered the day we met, changing me forever. I love you with all the recesses of my being. Thank you for being an amazing father and a supportive partner.

ON FIRE

*I*t's an impossible question to answer. How can I choose when I've just escaped from a place that has given me no choice? I feel trapped in a situation of my own making. The choice to be here and take this chance is all on me. I just hope that I haven't fucked this whole thing up.

We escaped the Light only to still be forced into a position to harm others. As the Changer, they expect me to choose sides, but I know the right thing is to make them both suffer. Monarchs have ruled Faerie and Earth for too long. It's time I use my Changer powers for good.

My Arion, Red, and mate, Cass, are one hundred percent behind me, but they don't know my full intentions. I can't tell them yet because I have to figure out how to get us out of this mess I created. Grey and Logan have been dragged into a world they didn't choose, and Grey's hatred for the Fae is clouding his judgment.

Looking into the eyes of the Queen, I become overwhelmed with the need to run. She's not going to like my answer, and I'm afraid I don't have a choice. Either comply or get killed. I have too many people I'm responsible for. Glancing over at Logan, I see his sweet face and know he doesn't deserve any of this. He shouldn't have to shoulder all this violence and cruelty.

"I cannot choose," I tell the Queen. She stares at me for a moment in disdain. I don't think many people defy her, and I'm bringing all sorts of trouble to her doorstep.

"Let me make this perfectly clear, Azrael of Earth. You don't have a choice. You came to my realm and asked for help. You're here because you are looking for sanctuary, not because you chose to come into the lion's den. You will obey me, or your pet here will suffer the consequences," she says to me in a demanding tone. She is inching closer to Grey as she speaks. I turn my attention to him, and he's frozen in time. His eyes are running wild, but he can't move his body.

"What are you doing to him?" I yell. Grey and I don't have the best relationship, but I would never want to see him hurt. Logan tries to step closer to his brother, but Cass holds him back and whispers something in Logan's ear.

"I thought you would have figured it out already. I'm not here to play games. It's acceptance or death. You either choose to accept your Changer fate and train with my men to battle the Light, or Grey becomes mine, and you all get to die a slow death in my dungeons. Cassiel is immortal; do you want to find out if you are too?" she asks me with a sly smirk. Her lips are pulled up at the corner of her mouth. She's amused by my lack of confidence in my Changer abilities, and by the kingdomless prince.

I grit my teeth and stare into her face. Reaching out through our bond, I channel Cass in my mind. *What do we do?*

We go along with what she says, Azra. This is not something she will negotiate on. We are stuck. I'm so sorry. This is all my fault, he projects back to me. I can feel his sorrow and his pain through the mating bond. He thought he was doing the right thing.

This is on me though. I'm the one who chose to agree and lead us all here. It is my responsibility to get us out. "I accept your terms. Now, let Grey go," I say.

A light sparks in her eyes as she envisions the potential that this may bring. She is reveling in the death and destruction that will come from my choice.

She turns then and walks over to the throne, releasing Grey as she goes. You can hear his gasps as he bends over to catch his breath. She calls forth two jaguars with a flick of her hand. It's a movement I notice only because my fear of what she could do next has me focused on her and nothing else in the room. They come to her side quickly, their black coats shining in the light. One is bigger than the other, with hidden spots along his body. His muscles ripple as he heads down the stairs to us. As he approaches me, he immediately walks into my personal space. My body freezes and a cool rush of adrenaline fills my veins. I want to move away, but I'm cemented in place by fear. He looks into my eyes, and I swear I pee a little.

Just before my heart fails me, a shimmer of light appears, and a man stands in the jaguar's place. I should be used to all the weird shit that goes on around here, but to see a naked man where a jaguar once was is pretty shocking. And what a man he is. He's tall and broad in the shoulders with muscles sculpting his body. Tattoos cover both of his arms, intricate designs I want to trace with my fingers. His hair is dark as pitch, and his eyes are a violet so bright, they remind me of amethysts. His jaw is chiseled, and he has a five o'clock shadow dusting his face. He's the dark to Cass's light, and though I feel a bit guilty, I can't look away. I'm enraptured.

"Azrael," he says my name like a prayer. His eyes roam all over me, and it sends a shiver along my spine. My eyes dark to his lips, and I lick my own in response. The heat that he is giving off pulls my body towards his, and before I know it, I'm standing toe to toe with a man I don't even know.

"Who are you?" I ask, breathless. Because I need to call him something. I must know more about him.

"Shax, son of Lucifer, heir to the Unseelie Court throne," he says, his voice thick like honey, coating me and giving me butterflies in my stomach. His eyes don't leave my face. There are people all around us, but they mean nothing at this moment. He is all-consuming, and the rest of the world disappears. The pull to him is stronger than any I have felt before. I need to feel him touching me in any way possible. The draw has me inclining my head towards him, and he leans down and touches his lips to mine. The kiss is gentle and soft, giving me feelings of completeness. He tastes like sin and darkness. I can think of nothing else but to be one with him. I throw myself at him. I have no idea why I'm acting this way. I'm aware that Cass is next to me, but I'm not getting anything from the mating bond. He's not sad or jealous; if anything, he is amused.

Shax picks me up to meet his large frame, and my feet are dangling above the floor. There's so much heat in his kiss and his body, that I feel as if I might combust. My skin feels prickly, and the intensity keeps growing. I run my fingers through his hair and give it a gentle tug. He moans into my mouth with a deep grumble. I bring my legs up and wrap them around his waist; feeling his rock-hard manhood underneath me. Rocking into him, it causes him to push closer. Awareness returns to me that we aren't alone. Pulling back from the kiss, I stare into his eyes. I notice two things at that moment, one—he's my alpha mate, and two—we are on fire. The bond is singing through my veins, telling me he is mine. It feels so right.

I jerk my body down from his and see my whole body is engulfed in flames. I start to yell, but I can't hear anyone over the raging of the flames. I don't move for fear that I'll hurt someone. "You need to calm down, Azrael. Take a deep breath and focus on my voice," Shax says. He's standing next to me in the fire. He's not getting burned, but rather, repelling my flames with his own. His flames are blue like freshly frozen water. Mine are red and orange, the color of the sun. When they mix, they form a violet blaze similar to his eye color. It's hypnotic and beautiful.

I take a deep breath and try to focus on his face, his beautiful face. The roaring dies down, and I can finally see my surroundings. Shax is holding onto my hand. The ground around us is charred and everyone, including the queen, is standing on the other side of the room.

"Well, isn't this a pleasant turn of events!" she laughs out in a raised voice. She has a smile from ear to ear. "This definitely makes you Dark, Azrael," she says as she approaches us. She notices the handholding and her grin gets ever wider. "Mating with the son of a Queen—only a Dark can accomplish this."

"My name is Azra," I tell her through gritted teeth. She's starting to piss me off with her inappropriate smiles and pretty hair.

"Azra. I like it. Makes you sound like less of an angel and

more of a demon," she says with a wink, making her way back to the giant door she arrived from. "Make sure you take your mate to her quarters, son. I trust you to explain the rest to these peasants."

With that last flick of her dress, she is gone. The doors close and silence rings throughout the room. I glance over at Cass who has a grim look on his face. Grey is holding Logan back, who looks like he is ready to run. I look up at Shax and give him a tight smile before walking away and approaching the guys.

"Cass," I say in a pleading tone. I don't know how I'm going to explain this. I reach out for his hand, and he clasps it in his. He pulls me toward him and crushes me to his chest. He smells like rain and thunder.

"I know, Azra. I felt it in the bond when he joined. We're his mates, and he's the alpha. I always knew it wasn't me, but I never expected you would have two heirs in your harem," he tells me. He has love in his voice and in his heart. I can feel that he is not sad or angry. He is just disappointed.

"Why are you not upset?" I ask him. I pull away from his chest so that I can look into his grey eyes. There is a storm raging behind them. He wants me, right then and there. He wants to stake his claim and demand Shax know I'm his as well, but he knows we have to wait.

"Being the Changer allows you certain benefits. One of them is having a harem of men to protect, guide, and love you. I knew I would not be your only, but I just didn't think you had Dark in you," he says.

"I don't have Dark in me," I exclaim, looking around at all the men here. But I'm lying to myself. I can feel the pull to this court just as I did the Light. Grey is not looking too good, and Logan appears scared. We need to bring this somewhere else, somewhere we all can rest.

"You do, actually," Shax says from behind me. "If you didn't, we wouldn't have been mated. It's even more unusual that a kiss was all it took for us to mate. Normally, I would have had to fuck you to get the kind of power we just gave off."

"Great. Another thing to add to the growing pile of shit Azra can do," I say with an exasperated sigh.

"Can you please show us to our quarters?" Cass says to Shax. "We've been traveling for a couple of days and need to clean up and sleep. Also, a meal would be nice."

"Right away, Your Highness," Shax says, with a mocking tone and a little bow. He winks at me and turns to leave. "Follow me."

Only then do I realize that he's still completely fucking naked, and I'm staring at his ass. Holy hot damn, that's a nice ass. Oh, the things I want to do to this man. My thoughts are interrupted by a crushing hug behind me.

"I'm so glad you are ok, Az. I was so worried when you caught on fire. I mean, you were like a ginormous fireball! It was cool, but a little scary too," Logan says into my back. I can feel the tension in his hug. He must have been frightened by all that just happened.

I turn around and kneel in front of him. "I'm sorry I scared you. I didn't mean to. These powers are all new to me, and I'm trying to figure them out. It took even me by surprise," I say, as I brush a lock of his hair across his forehead. He's so small and so innocent.

"I know you don't do these things on purpose, but you have to admit they sure do happen a lot. Maybe you want to try to not get into any more trouble," he says as he leans in to give me another hug. He whispers into my ear, "I thought Greyson was going to cry when you did that. He was very upset. I'm pretty sure he likes you."

I can't help it, I let out a laugh. This kid is too smart for his own good. Standing up, I offer him my hand. We start to walk toward where Shax went with the others. I guess we should rest and then figure out our next move.

RECHARGE

*S*hax leads us to a suite on another floor. There's one large sitting room and then four bedrooms branching off from the center. Like the throne room, these rooms are done in blacks and purples. It's all very noir. There's a sectional couch with a coffee table and matching recliner. The fireplace takes up one wall and looks like a giant dragon's mouth. The draperies are thick and dark, but I can still see a stream of light cracking through. Cass walks over to the windows and pulls them open for more light.

"I need a shower and a meal," I turn around and say to the guys. I'm exhausted and could sleep for a year.

"I'll have the staff bring up something for you," Shax says with a little nod as he goes back out the way we came.

As soon as he leaves, Grey is on me in a second, "What the fuck was that, Azra? Another mate? How many Fae are you going to collect? If you hadn't noticed, we aren't doing too good here. Now you got us mixed up with the Dark!"

"It's not like I planned any of this, Grey! I'm just as much of a victim here. I didn't want any of this. And let me remind you, you're the fucking reason why we are all here. Makes you wonder what would have happened if you just had walked away," I yell at him. I'm so done with all of this. I stomp off toward the closest bedroom door. I feel a bit bad for throwing that in his face, but it's the truth. I'm sick of him always blaming things on me.

It's a simple room, but it looks like there's an adjoining bathroom, so that's where I head. I find a place for my sword in a chest that's tucked into the back by the vanity. I strip out of my nasty clothes and run the shower. I'm a mess. My long black hair is matted in some places, my skin is pale, and my grey eyes look washed out. Rubbing my hands over my face, I start to think about all the shit that just happened. This is a fucking nightmare. I was so desperate to get away from Michael, that I didn't even realize what we might be getting ourselves into here.

Turning on the shower, I step into the spray and let the hot water cascade down my tired muscles, sighing as the tension leaves from the heat. Quickly, I wash my hair and body. I try and relax my mind, letting everything go as I do, but there is just so much. Noli is stuck with that bastard, and I couldn't save her. What if he's torturing her? I could never live with myself if she was harmed. All of this is because of me. I can feel the sting of tears in the back of my throat. The last week comes crashing around me, and I let out a pained cry. Clutching the wall and resting my head on it, I let out all the emotions I've been holding in. I cry for my old life and for the lives of all the others I've dragged into this. I cry for Logan because he's so young and innocent. I cry because it seems impossible to think we can get out of here alive.

"Are you ok?" Cass asks. He has the door of the shower open, and he's looking at me with such pity.

"No, I'm not. I don't know what to do, Cass. I'm afraid I

fucked this whole thing up," I tell him, wrapping my arms around my waist and hugging myself.

He undresses quickly and steps into the shower. He grabs me and pulls me into his chest. I smell his calm winter scent right away. He smells like snow-capped mountains and ice-covered berries. I grab him and try to push myself against his body more than I already am. I really let it out then. I'm practically screaming by the time he pulls me out of the shower and dries me off, wrapping me in a large fluffy towel. Doing the same for himself, he lays us on the chaise lounge in the corner of the room. He doesn't break contact as he positions us. He holds me tighter and hugs me until I slip into a deep sleep.

I wake up on the chaise in the same spot. I've got cotton stuck to the top of my mouth and a pounding headache. I look up and see him staring right at me.

"Hey, do you feel better?" he asks. He looks so concerned. I know I must look a fright.

"Somewhat. I think that being here with you has helped," I say as I smile up at him. His face is so close to mine. I rub my cheek against his and stare into his eyes. He brings both of his arms up around me and starts to caress my back. The spot between my shoulder blades has always been super sensitive for me. I put my hands in his hair and pull him toward me. Our kiss is soft and sorrowful. It's everything I don't want it to be, but everything I need. Sitting up I straddle him, increasing the intensity of the kiss. My tongue finds his and we fight for dominance. This isn't like the kiss with Shax. That kiss set my soul on fire; this kiss is about comfort. Cass is my balm, my rock, my constant in all the insanity. He's the one holding everything together. He may not be my alpha, but he's the reason this all works.

I move my hand down in between us and remove my

towel. I shimmy backward and open his up like a present. I don't think I will ever get used to the fact that this man is mine, forever. His cock is at attention, and I'm gifted with the glorious site. He's such a handsome man, but when I get to see all of him, it's a hundred times better. I slowly jerk him up and down. His hands are now on my breasts, playing with my nipples. My strokes become more urgent as I think of all the things, I want to do to him.

"Let's move this to the bedroom," I tell him. "I don't want to have sex on this chaise."

He doesn't respond but just picks me up and walks us out into the bedroom. He tosses me onto the bed and is on top of me in an instant. His mouth is all over my body, sucking and kissing his way down to my core. I was never a fan of oral sex, but something about Cass makes me want to be wrong. He kisses my inner thighs before he reaches my center. His warm mouth covers my clit and flicks his tongue out licking it, once, twice, and then on the third he takes the whole of it in his mouth and sucks. I arch my back on the bed and lace my fingers through his hair. I bite down hard on my lip and enjoy all the sensations coursing through my body.

"Oh, Cass," I moan into the pillows. He must take this as encouragement because he raises his left hand and slips two fingers inside of me. He matches his pumping with flicks of his tongue. I feel like I'm stuck in a vortex of pleasure. I wiggle and moan around him as he increases his speed and pressure. I'm not going to be able to hold on much longer. He adds a third finger, and I fucking lose it. I shatter, clenching my muscles and squeezing his fingers. I let out a moan that will definitely be heard by everyone.

"Hmm, that was amazing," I say to him after he picks his head up and looks into my eyes. He smiles and crawls on top of me. His kiss is passionate, and I feel like I need him closer. I flip us around and land on top of him. He doesn't question and I don't ask. I just line us up and slam down onto his cock, hard. Now it's his turn to groan. His eyes look like a lightning storm, as the streaks of power course through them. I start to move, feeling our connection through the bond, and it's singing with our passion. Nothing about this is slow or steady. I pick up the pace and soon we are both groaning and breathing to the rhythm that I'm setting. His eyes are glued to mine, like he can see into my soul. A spark of electricity leaves his fingertip and wraps around my nipple, zapping it. The mix of pain and pleasure sends a jolt of excitement up my body. He repeats this with the other nipple, and I bite down on my lip.

"You like a little pain, then?" he asks me with a look that could melt butter.

"I like anything you're going to give me," I tell him.

He wastes no time, flipping me over and entering me from behind. He grabs my hair and starts to plow into me so hard that we move the bed. His thrusts are erratic and animalistic. It's everything that we have gone through in the last few days being worked out. He's trying to gain some of the normalcy he craves. I can feel the pressure of an orgasm building, so I reach down and start to massage my clit. He releases my hair and grabs ahold of my voluptuous hips. His hands are digging into me, and I feel his need to come growing closer.

Removing my hand from my clit, I take a play from his book and release a bit of my own electricity down my hand wrapping it around his balls. When he hits the next thrust, I zap him a bit. He grunts at my effort, but I guess it wasn't enough. I try with a little more, and I'm granted with a delicious moan that almost matches my own. We erupt in a symphony of pleasure as I tighten up around him, milking his cock to get every last drop.

We lie there for a while in silence, just relaxing and letting our minds come down from that incredible high. His presence is so strong and so solid. I don't know what I would do without him. Sean was my everything for so long, but Cass...he's the cosmos. He makes sense in all of this nightmare reality.

There is a knock on the door, and before I can respond, Shax walks right in. I would go and cover myself, but really, there's no point. As my mate, he can feel my thoughts and desires. He would've already known that we were in here together.

"Come right in," I say to him in a sarcastic tone. Raising up on my elbows, I get a better look at him. He's put on some clothes, which fit him like a glove—dark blue jeans with a bright white t-shirt. It's so tight across his chest you can see his perky nipples. He smells like campfire and fall nights. His hair's damp, and his eyes are shining like two bright jewels. I can feel his arousal from here.

"I wanted to see if you were hungry," he says to me with a smile. I don't miss the up and down look he gives Cass either. He likes what he sees. This sets off a naughty train of thoughts in my head of the two of them inside me at the same time. I must not have done a good job of keeping that to myself because Shax's grin gets wider, and I hear Cass choke next to me.

"We'll be out in a second," I tell him as I get my wits about me. I hop off the bed and go into the bathroom and freshen up. Gods, the two of them are going to be the death of me.

J step out into the living room and find everyone gathered, enjoying a meal together. Cass saved me a seat next to him, so I go and sit down. Logan is shoveling piles of food in his mouth like he hasn't eaten in three years. Grey is picking at his plate while Cass and Shax are deep in conversation. This isn't how I pictured them acting. They're being so civil and polite to one another. I wonder if they're really getting along or if it's just their princely manners. I'm so used to Grey's abrasive behavior that I expect all men to act like that towards each other.

"So, what's the plan now?" I ask the table. They all stop what they're doing and turn to look at me. Suddenly, I have everyone's attention.

Shax breaks the silence first. "We train. You heard my mother. It's either get on board or get dead, and I would really like to get to know you first before we are executed."

"What are we training for, exactly? You see, no one has ever told me what it is I need to do," I tell him. I'm curious to see if he's going to blow me off just like Cass did in the beginning.

"You're going to train to use your magic. I'm going to teach you about using your fire powers and Cassiel is going to show you how to use your lightning and air. We don't know if you'll have any other mates or if you're going to gain any other skills, so we can start there," he says to me.

"What about Grey and Logan? What'll they do?" I ask Shax. He seems to enjoy his alpha role. I want to see if he'll treat everyone fairly, or if he's going to be a snobby prince.

"Greyson trains with us, learning basic fighting and sword skills, and Logan here, well, he gets to go to school," Shax says with a giant smile directed toward the boy.

"School? No way! I am not going to school. I am not a

Fae. I can't go to their schools. They'll bully me. Azra! Don't make me go!" he yells to the point where there are almost tears in his eyes. To an eleven-year-old boy, this must seem like the end of the world.

"Wolvie, if there is a chance for you to get an education, then you need to go. I'll make sure there are no bullies that bother you. The Dark seems to be different than the Light. Besides, you are best friends with the Changer, so they might show you some favoritism," I tell him. I wasn't a fan of school either, but it is important he catch up on his studies.

"As much as I hate leaving you with these Fae, it's something you should be doing. It's been too long since you learned anything, and I don't want my little brother to be uneducated because of my mistakes," Grey says, looking guilty. He still blames himself for getting taken.

"Ugh, you guys make some sense, but just know I don't like it. And if anyone bullies me, I'm stopping. I won't go back. I don't want to be a victim anymore," he says, looking away from us. I can see a bit of tears in his eyes. I need to change the subject.

"When do we start?" I ask Shax.

"Tomorrow. Today we should tour the castle, and show you around, so you know where everything is. Also, the three of us need to talk," he says, pointing to Cass and me.

"About?" Cass asks with a raised eyebrow. I don't think he's going to be submissive to my alpha.

"We need to discuss our bond. I've seen it get complicated if the rules are not laid down right away," he tells us.

"Shax, I know that we have only known each other for a short amount of time, but I'd like to clarify something here and now," I tell him, with a fierce look on my face. There's no way I'm letting this get too far. "I'm not, nor will I ever, be under someone else's command. This is not a monarchy. We will work as a team, so you demanding things from me isn't going to work."

He looks at me with a smile that could set the room on fire. His whole face has lit up, and I can tell he's amused with me. He's so handsome at this moment, it's taking all of me not to reach over the table and pull his mouth toward mine.

"I would never think to control you, my mate. I'm only suggesting we get certain dynamics out of the way before we proceed with this relationship. It's going to be a bumpy road ahead, and I want to make sure you have a solid foundation to lean on," he explains with that smoldering face of his. He could be an underwear model.

"Oh. Well, in that case, I agree. We should sit down and talk. I'd like Grey to be in on the conversation as well," I say to him. I quickly look down at my plate and start shoveling food in my mouth. I don't want to see any of their expressions. Even though I know Grey isn't mine, I feel responsible for him. I need to make sure he's included so I can keep an eye on him. I have this gut feeling he's going to be important.

"I don't need to be in on your kinky sex life. I want nothing to do with any of you. I'm only here because I needed to get the fuck out of the Light. So, don't include me in any of your plans. That goes for you too, *cat*. I don't want to train with you," Grey spits out. He's pissed again. I need to get him alone so we can have a chat and hash out all his anger. I'm starting to get fed up with his constant bad-mouthing.

"Let me be very clear here, *human*, you don't have a choice. We may be more lenient here, but we don't give free rein. If you want to survive, you need to bite your tongue, and do as you are told. Azra's in charge, whether you are on board or not," Shax says. He doesn't look like someone you'd want to make mad, especially after the little fire show we just produced.

In true Grey fashion, he gets up from the table and storms off. Logan looks torn between his brother and the rest of us. He's looking at the door his brother left through, almost like he's embarrassed by Grey's actions. I don't think everyone understands how much this kid really does take in. He must have such stress on his shoulders.

"Logan, you can go to Grey if you want. Don't feel like you need to sit with us. I know you're having a hard time with everything," I say to him in a gentle tone.

"It's ok. If I go in there, he's just going to yell at me anyway. When he gets like this, it's better to leave him alone. He's always had an anger problem," he says, looking a bit sad.

"Shax, can you introduce Wolvie to any other children?" I ask. Maybe if Logan finds a friend his mood will improve.

"There are quite a few of them. We even have something like a rec center here. When the kids aren't in school, most Fae parents can't be bothered with their offspring, so they send them there to get rid of them for the day," he says, with a sorrowful expression. It seems like he might have first-hand knowledge of that.

"How about we go and take a walk over there once we finish up here?" I ask Logan.

"I guess, but I think we need to ask Greyson if I can go. He gets pissed when I don't tell him where I am," he says to me. He doesn't look thrilled by the idea, but I think part of him misses having friends.

"Want me to go ask him?" I offer, giving him a sympathetic look.

"Would you? He's just gonna yell at me," he says, sheepishly picking at something imaginary on the table.

I get up and walk toward the bedroom Grey disappeared through. I knock on the door, but there is no answer. I try the handle and find it unlocked. Opening up the room, I walk in. The decor is similar to my own. There are light blue walls to accent the cream-colored furniture. Sconces are lit, giving off a romantic glow, and the carpet is plush under my feet. I hear the groan of a door and look up to see Grey coming out of what I can only assume is the bathroom. He's dressed in nothing but a towel. My mouth pops open as I stare at all his handsomeness. His muscles are lean and defined. His blond hair is plastered to his head, and when he sees me, his nostrils flare in anger.

"What the fuck, Azra!?" he yells, but doesn't make a move to cover up or change. This brings me out of my trace because I blink a bunch of times before I reply.

"Sorry, I just umm...I needed to ask you something, and you weren't answering."

"Obviously, I was in the shower. What do you want?"

"I want to take Logan to the rec center, but wanted to check with you if it was cool?"

"No, I'll go with you."

"I don't think that's a good idea. You nearly just flipped the fuck out in there. The kid knows you're mad all the time, and it shows. He's sad, Grey. Can't you see that?"

"I... I know that. I'm trying my best here. I have no fucking idea what I'm doing. It's just this place. All this is fucking infuriating," he says, exhaustion apparent in his eyes.

"Why don't you cool off and rest, and I'll bring Logan? I'll make sure he's taken care of. Please, he needs this," I beg,

I'm not above it. Logan needs a break from all this adult drama.

"Fine, but you better bring him back in one piece, or I'm going to hold you responsible," he says, giving me a pointed look.

"Gotcha. We'll be back sometime later on," I reply, leaving the room and returning back to the guys.

We eat the rest of our meal talking about different topics. Shax wants to know about everything on Earth, as he has never been, and Cass wants to know about the rest of Faerie. I listen to both sides and chime in when necessary, but my mind is on the Queen's motives. We need to figure a way out of this fucking mess, and I need to do it quickly. My other thoughts stray to Shax. I need to know where his loyalties lie. Cass was quick to get rid of his father. I don't blame him, but will Shax do the same? I don't intend to fight for Light or Dark. I worry about how the boys will take that bit of knowledge.

3

FINDING LOGAN, A FRIEND

*T*he rec center turns out to be a stadium full of kid activities. There are different courts that look just like basketball, tennis, and handball, but a bit different. A full-sized football type field is behind the building and an Olympic-sized heated swimming pool on the ground floor. Logan's eyes light up as we enter the building. There are quite a few children here of all different ages.

Shax and I escort Logan. I left Cass behind to babysit Grey and make sure he didn't get into any trouble. There's only so much I can take of his attitude. I don't need him to go and start making trouble.

"I'll introduce you to one of the counselors, Logan. She'll be able to introduce you to some children that will be in your class, and you can get a feeling of how things work," Shax says, in a gentle tone. He really is trying to include Logan, which is melting my heart a bit.

"Alright, but I need to know where you guys are going to be, just in case these kids are assholes," Logan says with an exasperated sigh.

"Language!" I say, because, fuck, the kid is eleven.

"Sorry, but it's true. What if I hate everyone and then I am stuck here?" he whines.

"You're right," I say. Turning to Shax I ask, "Do you have anything like cell phones here? Maybe a few carrier pigeons or owls?"

"We have burn pages," he says, like I am supposed to know what that means. He must see the confusion on my face because he explains, "They are pieces of paper that are spelled to be carried to the receiver and once they are opened, they combust. It's a very effective way to get a quick message to someone."

"So cool! How do I do it? Will you show me?" he asks, while jumping up and down a bit. The kid looks like he's vibrating from so much excitement.

"Let's talk to your counselor, Anna, first and see if she can show you around a bit. Then we can talk about the burn pages," Shax says to him. He's a natural at this. I wonder if he's taken care of children before.

We walk up a few flights of stairs and come to a wing that looks like it holds a bunch of offices. Shax leads us to one of the doors and knocks. "Come in!" yells a female voice.

Shax opens the door, and a beautiful woman around my age looks up and smiles at us. Her gaze immediately turns toward Shax, and I feel a pang of jealousy as she takes him in. My body angles in front of him on instinct, and I can hear the soft chuckles behind me. Apparently, I'm funny.

"Relax, mate. Anna is taken," Shax says as he places a gentle hand on my shoulder and squeezes. He gives me a smile and a look that says I-can't-wait-for-later.

"Mate? What did I miss?" Anna says.

"It was sudden, but yes, we are mates. This is Azrael the Changer," Shax tells her. She's shocked. Her eyes roam over us, and her hand goes to her mouth as if she's covering a gasp. Whether about the mating or me being the Changer, I have no idea.

"That's amazing," she says. I can tell she wants to say more, but Logan is starting to get antsy. She notices him then and offers a brilliant smile.

"This is Logan. He's my friend and under my protection. We're wondering if you would be able to show him around a bit, maybe introduce him to a few friends? He's going to be starting school here, and I'd like for him to feel as welcome as possible," I tell her with a stern look. She needs to know Logan's important.

"Of course! I'd love to serve as your guide, Logan. I have a few kids in mind who would be perfect. They're all very well behaved and work with the younger kids when I need some help.

"Ok, but I want to know how to use burn pages in case I need to see Azra. I don't want to be stuck here if this sucks," he tells Anna.

"I see His Highness let you in on our little secret. He only does that for people he likes, so you must be a very important guy," she says. I like her a little more now. Logan should be made to feel special, and I'm glad we are on the same page.

"Anna, can you take it from here? I need to show Azra some other areas of the palace grounds before we start training tomorrow," Shax asks.

"Of course. Come on, Logan. Let's go see if we can find the students I was talking about," she says as she gently places an arm around his shoulders. She leads him out the door, but before he's gone, he turns around and looks at me. I know he's scared, but he's putting on a brave face.

"See you in a bit. Have fun," I tell him as I wave.

Shax turns to me then and does the unexpected. He pulls me into his arms and places his mouth on mine in a hungry display of passion. I return his kiss with vigor. His lips are soft as they explore every inch of my mouth. He runs his tongue across my lips, and I part them more for him. He feels divine, sending shockwaves of anticipation all over me. I step in closer and plaster my body onto his. He's so much taller than me, that my neck is bent up to reach him.

I break the kiss long enough to stare up into his eyes and say, "Where is it that you wanted to take me?"

"My bed," he says, with a purr. He kisses along my jawline up to the shell of my ear. He whispers, "My only intention is to see you naked for the rest of the afternoon. That's the only tour I will be taking you on."

My knees give out a little, and my whole-body quivers in anticipation. Shax is beautiful, but his commanding voice and his kindness to Logan has me spun up tighter than a yo-yo. I want this man with every fiber of my being, and I will have him now.

"Take me. I want to spend time exploring you. I need to feel you inside of me," I say to him. His eyes widen, and his cock hardens on my stomach. If this was his private office, I don't think we would have waited.

"Let's go, then, my firefly," he says, with a wink and a quick kiss. I don't know if I like being called a bug, but there's just something about Shax that would make me do just about anything.

He places his arm across my back and squeezes me further in. Before I can even question him, we are sucked into a vortex and dumped out on the other side. My body feels like it has been torn apart and put back together the wrong way. What the hell just happened? I'm so dizzy, that I can't even identify my surroundings. I collapse onto the floor and wait for it to subside.

"Shit, Azra. Are you ok? I thought you knew how to teleport," Shax says, getting down to my level on the floor. I'm lying on something soft. It feels extra cushiony on my throbbing head.

"Are you fucking kidding me?" I ask him. "I didn't even know anyone could teleport until a minute ago."

He looks at me a bit sheepishly, "I'm sorry, I didn't know." I feel bad for snapping at him, but holy hell, my head hurts. Giving it a few minutes, I wait patiently until my brain stops throbbing. I begin to look around the room and notice we're in his bedroom, or so I gather. It's cozy in here. A four poster bed lines one wall, while there's a roaring fire on the opposite side. His furniture is classic, like you'd see in an older home. The rug which I'm currently laying on is plush and white. I can feel the softness of it on my cheek.

After a few minutes, I tentatively get up and look around. Behind me, there's a chest of drawers and a desk. Papers are scattered everywhere. "Nice room," I say.

"Thanks. Are you feeling alright? Do you want water?" he asks. I nod my head, and he rushes off to the side of the room where there's a wet bar with various pitchers and bottles of liquids. He returns with the water and hands it to me. I enjoy the taste of it going down. They must put some sort of mint in it—it's refreshing.

Walking on shaky legs, I use Shax as support on my way over to the bed. I lay down and stare up at the canopy that's draped above. It's a beautiful room. It reminds me of something from a romance movie, but it doesn't really fit Shax at all.

"Why all the frilly decor? I didn't take you for that kind

of guy," I say to him. I'm starting to feel better. My head is clearer, and I'm not in as much pain.

"This was my sister's room before she died. I couldn't bring myself to change anything. She was the true heir until she met her demise," he tells me, with a devastated look on his face. She must have meant a lot to him.

"What happened?" I ask. I know I'm being forward, but I need to know my mate. If he's going to be my alpha and my mate, we should be comfortable enough to share with one another.

"She was killed in battle. We had a feud with rebel outcasts, Fae who wanted to overthrow my mother. She's not always a good Queen," he says looking down at his quilt and picking an imaginary lint ball off of it. "My mother does some fucked up things, and my sister paid the price. Sola was a strong and fair Fae. She didn't agree with my mother and lead the rebels against her. She was killed for her efforts. She would've made an amazing ruler."

"I'm sorry you lost her. I would've loved to meet her," I say, because what else is there to say? Condolences sometimes hurt more than they comfort.

"It was a long time ago, but I try to keep her in my memory. That's why I can't bring myself to change anything."

"I understand. It's hard when you lose someone close," I say, with a forlorn look on my face. "I remember what it was like to lose my dad; the only person that ever cared for me when I was little, and now Noli." Gods, I wish she were here with me.

"Who's Noli?" he asks, turning to face me a bit.

"She's my best friend, and Michael has her. I dragged her into this mess, and she's paying the price. I'd do anything to have her with me," I reply, closing my eyes for a second. I don't want to cry.

"I brought you here to explore your body, and we get stuck talking about depressing shit."

"Who says we can't forget the past for a little while and get lost in each other? I know I could use a distraction from all of this, and you look like you'd be the perfect person to give it to me," I purr, in a seductive tone. I grab his shirt and pull him in for a kiss. It's gentle and sweet, something I would've never expected from an alpha, someone who has so much power. He pushes me further back onto the bed without breaking contact. We kiss and rub one another, exploring the curves and planes of our bodies. He leans into me more, crushing me into the mattress. Parting my legs with his knee, he settles in. Moving his body up and down, the friction from my clothes is making me so wet for him. Moaning into his mouth, I run my fingers up his back and into his hair. I tug on it and make him look at me.

"I want to see you naked again," I tell him. He smirks at me but does what I ask. Taking his time peeling off his clothes, he gives me a thorough show before standing naked at the end of the bed. He is fucking perfect. Every delicious muscle is outlined to perfection. He has a splatter of hair going from his belly button to his massive cock, and the best part—his arm tattoos. I noticed it before, because it was hard not to, but now I get to look at it in detail. Beautiful scroll work, mandalas, animals, and flowers grace both his arms in a picturesque design. The tattoo artist who did all of it is extremely talented.

"Now you," he says with a smoldering look in his eyes. He senses my arousal and can probably tell through the bond how much I desire him.

Kneeling on the bed, I take off all of my clothes, one

piece at a time, giving him the same show, he gave me. The chill in the air causes my nipples to harden and my skin to get goosebumps all over. He wastes no time joining me back on the bed, ready to fulfill my every need. Tongue and teeth clash as the need we have for one another increases. Shax is all consuming. We're breathing the same breath and the air around us is charged and ready to explode.

He enters me in one swift motion, and I buck on the bed, leaning back into the pillows. His hands run down my chest and stomach, squeezing and caressing as he goes. Finding my nipple, he takes it into his mouth and sucks while he rides me into oblivion. It doesn't take long for me to climax, and I let out a guttural moan to make sure he knows how much he pleases me.

He flips me around before I stop clenching and enters me from behind. His cock stretches my dripping pussy as he pumps into me in a frenzied state. I can't help but turn my head and look at this magnificent man. His hands are palming my ass as he glides in and out of me.

"Do you like to watch?" he asks, in a seductive tone. His head is cocked to the side in curiosity. I'm so turned on. Without saying a word, I reach down and start to play with my clit. His eyes go bright, and he licks his lips. "I'm going to taste you after I come inside you."

A thrill of desire pumps through my system, and I shatter around him again. My body is singing with power, and I feel the explosion of our mating rush over me. We're coated in flames — a wonderful mixture of blues and reds. Shax finds his own release in my orgasm and pushes deep within me as he finds his pleasure.

As promised, I'm turned around and laid on my back. Our fire is still alight, yet it isn't burning anything. I can feel the crackle of power running between us. "You're a magnificent creature, Azrael the Changer. I am beholden to your side for the rest of eternity. I bow down to you now in private but will pledge my loyalty to you in public. Allow me the gift of tasting your sweet pussy," he exclaims to me in such reverence that I have nothing to say and only nod in agreement. My eyes are tearing up, and I turn away, so he won't see.

He begins to lick and suck my clit, causing the already sensitive area to ignite in sensation again. He nips at my lips and thoroughly runs his tongue up and down the length of me. Tasting himself on me, a moan sounds from his lips which spurs me on even more. I grasp his hair and push his face more into my body. Taking this as a sign, he thrusts his tongue deep inside of me, fucking me with his mouth. His hand reaches up, and he starts to rub my clit in a steady motion. I bask in the passion he's giving me. I feel alive and godly. I don't last long. With one swift flick to my clit, I'm pulsing hard. Crying out his name, I collapse my legs on the bed. Gods, that was amazing.

As soon as we part, the fire goes out, leaving us in the warm glow of the fireplace. Turning to face one another, we stare into each other's eyes with silence between us. I trace the shape of his face with my hands and project what is in my heart. I'm lucky he's mine.

4

RED'S SECRET

$\mathcal{W}$e don't get dressed again for hours. Every time we stop, it is only minutes before we fall into each other's arms again. I can't believe how much my life has changed since I was brought into this world. I have two mates; men I can trust and share with. I feel guilty about keeping Shax in the dark, and it's finally time to let him in on our secrets. He should meet Red and get to know him better. As my alpha, I'm sure he will want to know my soul-bonded.

"Can you take me to the stables? I need to check on Red. I'd like for you to meet him as well," I say.

"Is that his name? He looks a lot like my Ash, except Ash is, well, the color of ash," he tells me, with a little chuckle. His face reveals the love he has for his horse. It has me curious if they will look alike. Red assured me he was the only one of his kind left.

I can't help but smile at him. He has a post-sex glow, and his hair is tousled from my hands running through it. His eyes are bright with lust, and I want nothing more than to pull him back in for another round.

Leaving the room, we walk out of the palace and head toward the stables. The grounds are magnificent. Large trees line the property, and there are beautiful flowers everywhere. Some I recognize, but others are too strange to not be from Faerie. Twisty vines hang from the stone castle, and the wall surrounding the garden. These trees are perfect to lay under and get lost in a book. Not too far from the grounds, there's a thick forest and a part of me wonders what's hiding or living there.

"This is beautiful," I say, looking up at Shax in amazement. He chuckles at me and places his hand in mine.

"What did you expect, fire and charred land?" he says, guiding us over to a path that I assume will take us to the stables.

"Honestly? Yes, I imagined the bowels of hell for the Unseelie Court," I say, with almost a straight face. A smile does pop out though, and that earns me another charming smile from Shax.

My body begins to buzz with excitement as we near the stables. I'm excited to see Red—I miss him. Thinking back on how they treated the horses at the Light, my stomach cramps with unease. I hope all the horses have been treated fairly, I'll go ballistic if something happened to them. Maybe I should have come sooner. Now I feel a bit guilty. His secret is so important though, so rushing to his side might have been suspicious.

Approaching the large building, I see a magnificent structure. It's just as stunning as it is in the Light, but there are Fae working here. I can tell by their energies that they are more than human. There are a few human stable hands, but no one looks distraught or downtrodden like in the Light. They look happy and enthusiastic in their work.

"Do you keep your horses in a separate section from the

rest?" I ask him, remembering how Red was classified as a companion horse.

"No, they're all mixed together. Wherever they are the most comfortable is where they fit. I imagine all your horses are together though. This keeps them from getting upset when they're separated from their friends," he explains. This is something I already know, so I just smile up at him.

Red will have the ability to keep them calm, even if there was a problem. "Tell me about Ash. I want to know everything," I say. He looks at me with a bit of mischief in his eyes.

"Ash was a present for my mother. Someone gifted her two horses that were identical, except for color. One was black and the other red. The red horse was lost in a battle many years ago. The black horse survived, and my mother gave her to me. She said that without the red one, she was useless. I didn't see it that way. She's always been my Ash. She's my soul-bonded horse who has been with me for over four decades. I'm forever grateful to her, as she's saved my ass a time or two," he tells me.

"She sounds wonderful. Red is also my soul-bonded. At first, I thought it was too good to be true to have a horse that could be connected to me like that, but after the ceremony, well, let's just say I would never consider being apart from him."

"Do you want to go for a quick ride? There's a waterfall that's not too far from here. We can take the horses, and then go get Logan right after," he asks me in an excited tone. I don't have the heart to tell him no.

"Alright, but we will have to be quick about it. I don't want to leave Logan for that long," I respond.

He tells me where to go and takes off in a jog to go tack up Ash. I make my way down the lane without him. I see

Red in the distance, he's in the last stall to the right. Storm and Hurri lean their heads out at my approach. I walk up to each of them and pat their cheeks. "Hey guys, how's it going down here?" I ask them.

Red leans his head all the way out and looks both ways before responding, "We have been treated fairly. They gave us food, water, and a groomsman came and bathed each of us. All is quiet on this side of the barn. From what I can gather, most horses are happy here."

"Thank gods. It's one less thing for me to worry about," I tell him reaching for his stall door. I swing it wide so that he's able to walk out. "Do you want to ride? Shax is getting his horse tacked. He wants to show me a waterfall."

"You have mated again. He is your Alpha," he says with no question in his voice.

"Yes, and I think you'll be happy to meet him. He's everything we need."

He seems to consider this; if a horse could look like he is considering something. His nostrils flare, and he swings his head around toward the way I just came. He moves so fast, that I can barely get out of the way when he swings his large body in a circle. I notice what has gotten him so riled up. Shax is coming down the hall with who I'm assuming is Ash, a horse just as big as Red, with a coat the color of smoke. She stops just as Red takes a few steps. They seem to be staring at each other. I try to get a read on his emotions, but he has shut me out.

Before I know what's happening, they are running toward each other. I cry out to Shax to get out of the way. Just before they collide, a shimmer of light overtakes them, and in their place are two humans, one male, and one female, both stark naked. They grasp onto each other and seem to try to consume one another with a passionate kiss.

"Holy fucking shit!" I yell from my place behind them. My Arion just turned into a man. A real man!

Red pulls away from Ash and turns to face me. I blush and hold out my hand to cover my eyes, "Red, you need to put some fucking clothes on," I say.

"Sorry, Azra," he replies, just before there's another pull of energy that I feel in my gut. I slowly peel my hand away and look at the sight before me. Both Red and Ash are now fully clothed.

"You want to explain to me what's going on?" I ask him. He looks at me a little sheepishly as he grabs Ash's hand. They stand together in solidarity. He looks to her, and she nods to him in reassurance.

"Ashlyn is my mate. We're the last Arions in existence, or so I think. We were separated when I was given to the Light as a spy. We haven't seen each other since," he says, pulling her into him some more and kissing her head. She has tears in her eyes. I don't think I could imagine being separated from Cass, or now Shax, for so long. My heart pangs for them.

"You've got to be shitting me," Shax says, speaking for the first time since all this has happened. "You're an Arion? Why didn't you tell me? We're soul-bonded, Ash. We have been for over 40 years!" He looks distraught. This is a big secret to keep from him.

"Shax, it wasn't like that. It's just... I didn't think I would ever see Redael again. I thought he was lost to me. I didn't want to bring that kind of attention to you or me. If your mother knew what we were, I would be ripped away from you," she exclaims in a beautiful voice. It sounds like a sweet melody.

Shax is having none of it. He walks over to me and stands beside me in a show of solidarity. He is showing her that she's not the most important to him any longer. A look of hurt crosses her face, and she turns her sad eyes to Red. Giving me a sympathetic look, he then turns toward his mate and kisses her head.

"Red, we need to talk. You need to explain what's going on. This has just been one cluster-fuck after another. I don't think my heart can take much more of this," I say, almost angry. I'm starting to get the same feeling I had in New York —things are too complicated, and it would be easier to run away and start over. Being the Changer is starting to become too much.

"Azra," he says, moving over to me and leaving Ash standing alone for a moment. He's not dismissing her but coming and giving me what he feels I need; grabbing me and pulling me in for a giant hug. He feels like safety and coming home. His smell is different; he isn't musk and beast any longer. He smells of blood and earth; like magic remade.

I return the hug and sigh into him. He's my soul-bonded Arion. There's nothing quite like this bond. Speaking into my mind for the first time since our ceremony he exclaims, *I'm sorry that I did not tell you. It was such a painful memory. Being split up was the worst thing that had ever happened to me. She is my heart, as you are my soul. There is never a second mate for an Arion.*

Why didn't she tell Shax she was an Arion? I ask.

Because she was afraid. Afraid for his life and hers. The Queen is a true ruler in what she does, her kingdom always comes first. We have great power alone, but together we are nearly unstoppable. We hid before our capture. I have been in my horse form ever since then.

Ash and Shax don't have the same type of soul-bond Red and I have. I'd have been able to tell through the mating bond if someone else was connected to us by the bond.

Stepping out of Red's embrace, I turn to face Shax. He stands there with a look of confusion in his eyes. He doesn't know that he never actually completed the bond.

"You need to complete your bond," I tell him. He raises his eyebrow in a sexy way that makes me want to forget this whole thing happened and crawl back into his bed.

"We did, decades ago," he responds, looking confused.

"Well, actually, we did not. I left out a few steps. I couldn't let them see what I was. You must understand that I was just trying to protect you. You are the second most important person in my life, and if you left or something happened to you, I would have died inside," Ash explains to him. Her sadness is coming through her energy, rolling off of her in grey waves. My heart breaks for her. I know what it's like to feel all alone, and not to be able to tell someone the whole truth. Noli pops into my mind, and my stomach clenches.

Shax's facade is cracking a little. He's so attached to her that her pain is his. I turn and look up at him. He sees the approval in my eyes and steps in front of me. He goes to her and they embrace. She begins to cry, and I want to reach out and console her. I can't imagine what she has gone through. She's such a strong Arion to be able to hold in the amount of pain she must have.

"They'll repair their bond," Red says to me. I can see the longing in his eyes, as he seeks out Ash. He wants to be alone with his mate. I don't blame him since it's been such a long time.

"Shax, why don't we pick up Logan and then go back to the room. We should let everyone else know what's going on," I say. He nods his head in agreeance before speaking. "When can we finish the ceremony? I don't like that we are not complete," he states, looking toward Ash.

"The full moon is tomorrow night. We can do it by the waterfall. It should be fairly quick because we already have our connection," she replies to him. He gives her a curt nod and reaches for my hand. He's still hurt from the secrets, but he can't help wanting to be whole with his soul-bonded.

"Are you ok?" I ask while we walk in the direction of the castle. I'm worried that he might fall apart. I know we're mates, but we've only known one another for a short time.

"Yes, and no. I didn't see that coming, that's for sure. I didn't think Arions still existed. They were said to be wiped out of existence ages ago. I also hate that she felt she had to lie to me. She was the only being in this realm that I fully trusted, and she'd been lying to me the whole time. She did an excellent job of hiding what she was. If I couldn't tell she wasn't a normal Fae horse; then no one could."

"She seems pretty special," I say. I want to take his worry away, but I just don't know how. This is all so new, and I'm not sure how he will react to my advice. He looks distraught, like his world has been flipped on his head.

"Do you think it's really the right thing to do? Telling the others," he asks. There is some trepidation in his voice.

After a brief pause, he continues, "You're right. I haven't had someone I can rely on in a long while. My sister was the only one I confided in, and she was taken from me. It's hard to let new people in. Our connection was so instant, so fast. It was like my body took over, and my mind has to play catch up. I hope you understand."

"I do, trust me. I haven't been exactly comfortable with all this either. I lived a simple life in a small town in Virginia before I was taken. Grey brought me into this world, and now I find myself with two mates, new identity, and a realm to save. It's a lot."

"I don't trust Greyson. He could be working with the

Light as a spy. He's so angry and doesn't listen to anything anyone says."

"Leave Grey to me. He will come around. He's been kidnapped, tortured, and made to work for the Light. Unfortunately, he doesn't know that there can be nice or good Fae. He's too caught up in his pain."

"I didn't know. I'm sorry he had to go through that. No one should have to live that way. I'm so glad we found each other. It really gives me hope for us all."

We walk in comfortable silence up to the suite. I'm feeling very overwhelmed thinking about the guys and the Queen. Shax seems equally caught up in his head. When the time comes, I wonder what side my mate will choose. The Queen wants my fealty, and I know I won't give it to her.

5

REMAKING GREYSON

*W*e get back into the room and find it empty except for Grey. There's food laid out on the table, and he's eating a plate while looking out the window. He doesn't notice us right away, which tells me he's in his own world, deep in thought. I walk up to him and sit down across from him.

"What's for lunch?" I ask, looking at the offerings on the table.

He shrugs. "I don't know what half of this stuff is, but the rolls are pretty good. There's some kind of meat that tastes like chicken, and there is a pink juice," he tells me plainly. Glancing over at him, I can see there's still so much pain in his eyes. I want to comfort him, but I know he'll reject it.

Making a plate, I look over at Shax. He's standing by the door, watching our interactions. "Aren't you going to sit down?" I ask, with curiosity in my voice.

"I think I'll go check on Logan. See how he's getting on," he says. His gaze tells me everything. He wants us to be alone to work it out. Grey tenses beside me.

"I'll go with you. I feel like shit for not being there in the first place," he says. It was unlike him to trust me with Logan, and the fact that he was ok with Shax being there really spoke to how much he was trying to control himself. He's feeling guilty for all that now.

"It's all good, he's a great kid. Stay and finish your lunch," Shax replies, leaving with a quick glance at me.

'Thank you' I mouth to him. The door shuts softly, and Grey turns to me. Our eyes meet, and there is so much to be said, but I've no idea where to start.

"Grey, I, um...we need to talk," I tell him. All of a sudden, I'm so nervous. He looks at me at that moment, and I swear he's trying to come up with a hundred different ways to either fuck me or kill me.

"What is it you want to talk about, Changer?" he asks. He says *Changer* like it's a dirty word.

"We need to talk about your role here. About what it means to all of us if you stay with us. I know you hate me, hate the Fae, but for the sake of your brother and for the sake of the world, you need to consider your options carefully."

"What options are those, Azra? Because from where I'm sitting, I have none. I can't go back to the Light, and I can't leave here either. There's no way Logan and I would last in Faerie by ourselves. As soon as we left, we would be killed or enslaved. I don't even want to know what lurks behind the castle walls," he tells me with trepidation in his voice. He is scared.

"I want you here with me," I say, truthfully. I'm attached to his grouchy ass, and I'd be crushed if he left.

"Why? So I can be your pet?" His anger is rising to the surface again. I need to get this under control before he walks off again.

"No, so you can be my friend. I want to forgive you for

what you did to me. I know that this isn't your fault, and I understand why you took me, but it's hard for me to fully trust you. We've been both hurt by the Fae, but that doesn't mean we can't try to get past it and maybe make a life. Logan is so vulnerable. I think he needs a safe place to stay, and this is the best we have to offer. I've come to care deeply for him. There's no going back for me. That boy has me wrapped around his finger."

I think I shocked him into stupidity because it takes at least ten seconds for him to respond. He doesn't say anything but moves around the table. "Tell me what you want me to do," he says. His voice is lower, and his eyes are holding something I have never seen from him before. Tenderness? Civility? I can't put my finger on it.

"I want for us to get out of here alive. I want to make sure that everyone back home is safe, and I want to separate Michael from his head. I want all of this, but I don't want to do it without you," I say. I'm not really sure where that all came from, but I know it's the truth. I want to make him see it's the truth, that I'll try to change things. That I'm just not another Fae making empty promises.

I get up from the chair and lean into him. Grey smells like peaches and cream. He has undertones of musk, and it's turning me the fuck on. I don't understand how I could be attracted to someone else. I already have two mates! But when I think about not having Grey around, a pang of sadness hits my chest.

"I'll see Michael dead. For all he's done to me and to the rest of the world," he says, with a tone so serious it sends chills up my spine. Given the opportunity, he would kill Michael. Anyone would.

"So, let's do it together. We're stronger as a unit. I'm just learning about all these powers I've accumulated, but I need someone to remind me who I was. I need a reminder that not too long ago, I was no one special. A human who was going about her business in life, trying to survive. Shax and Cass are great. They have awoken something inside me that I never thought possible, but I need someone to hold on to and anchor me back down to reality."

He considers me for a moment. I know he was hurt in the past. So was I, but we need to move on. Looking toward the future and accomplishing our common goal is all that matters. The past has to stay in the past.

"If I trust you, I'm going against everything I believe. Fuck, Azra! I want you, but I can't handle getting hurt again. I've been hiding my need through my anger. Every time one of them touches you, I wish it was me. I want to mark you, claim you as my own. I want to be inside you buried to the hilt, but I can't do that to Logan," he confesses. It smacks me in the face. I didn't think he'd ever admit it.

"Let me take your pain away for a bit. Let's see where this takes us. I would never hurt Logan. He's become too important to me. I love that kid already," I say, surprising myself. I feel the tug toward him, but I've been so busy with escaping and trying to keep us all safe, that I hadn't noticed how strong it was until now.

He breaks, and the next minute he's on me. His hands are rough as they thread through my hair. His lips are desperate and his kisses hot. I want him so bad in this moment. I want all of him, but I'll take this for now. His tongue enters my mouth, and we dance the fine line between dominance and acceptance. My hands run down his arms and along his chest. He's muscular, but not in the way a bodybuilder would be. This is from all his hard work —it's natural, and all Grey. He moans in my mouth a little as I lean in. I find the button of his jeans and start to undo the zipper. He removes his hands from my hair, and he places them on my shoulders. He slides them further in and before I know it, his hands are wrapped around my neck. A stab of worry goes through my system. How much do I really know about him? Before I can get too paranoid, he pulls away from the kiss.

"We need to take this into a bedroom before someone sees," he says breathlessly. He's so handsome at this moment, his blue eyes lit up with desire.

"What if I don't care if they see?" I reply. The look in his eyes blazes even more. He wants to be watched. Then realization hits him, and he says, "Logan."

"Let's go into my bedroom." I reach out for his hand, and before I know it, he has me flung over his shoulder in a fireman's carry. He smacks my ass, and I let out a squeal. Grinning to myself, I'm not going to tell him how much I enjoyed that.

He flings me on the bed and looks down at me, " I'm going to fuck you hard, Azra. This won't be sweet, and it won't be kind. I need to get this out of my system. Are you ok with that?"

My pussy clenches at his words. I feel wetness in my panties, and I nod my head.

"Say it. I need to hear you say it."

"I want you to fuck me, Grey. I want you to fuck me so hard that I come undone around you."

This is all the consent he needs. His clothes are stripped off in record time. I finally see all of him, and I am not disappointed. He is glorious. A true work of art.

I take off my clothes in a hurried fashion and watch his eyes run over my body. He must like what he sees, because his nostrils flare. He's on me in an instant. His mouth finds my breasts first. Sucking and nipping. He runs his hands over my stomach and finds out how wet I am when he gets to my apex. His hands feel so good on my skin that I arch back when he begins to make circling motions on my clit.

Running my hands through his hair, I give him a gentle tug to look at me. "Grey, I don't think I can take much more of this. I need you inside me, now," I whisper to him.

He responds with a kiss so passionate, that I almost come right there. His tongue invades my mouth as he readies himself to enter me. He takes a moment to tease me first, taking the tip and massaging it around my opening. The hardness of him against my soft folds sends a rush through my body. I feel like I could set the room on fire.

I make an impatient noise against his mouth, and he takes it as the signal to slam into me. His actions are intense. He's going to fuck me hard and not question it after. I can feel him start to lose control. I'm going to be the recipient of all his aggression, but I don't mind if this is what it takes to have Grey.

He grabs both of my hands and holds them above my head, while his thrusts become faster. I hook my legs around him to adjust the angle, and soon we are both panting. Looking up into his beautiful face, I see nothing but hurt. He still can't let go of everything that has happened. I want to hold him and tell him it will be ok for now, but I would be lying, and Grey doesn't need me to coddle him. He needs someone to fight.

Since my senses have been enhanced, thanks to Red, I wonder if my strength has as well. Without another thought, I flip us over, still attached, and start to ride him. His face has a look of pure shock when he sees what I can do, but it's so worth it. I give him everything I have, making him squeeze his eyes shut and almost come. His resolve strengthens, and he picks us up from the bed. He goes to flip me over when I shake my head, "I want to watch you come inside of me," I tell him.

His gaze gets more heated and angrier. He slams us against the wall. My legs are still wrapped around his waist as he fucks me into oblivion. My arms drape over his shoulders and he puts his head down into my neck.

His movements get more erratic as he pulls back and looks me in the face, "I hate that I want you so much," he says. His eyebrows are furrowed, and he is wearing his mask of pain. I take it for what it is. This is how he copes. This is how he is going to justify being with me.

I lick my lips and lean in, "Liar," I say to him as I slam my lips around his and dig my nails into his back. He groans into my mouth, and I can feel his body tense. I pull my head back and put his face in my palm. I need to see him let go.

He can't hold it much longer, and with another thrust, he comes undone, which has me pulsing around him. His whole face lights up, there's peace for a moment, and then the whole room is on fire.

Pure shock pulls me out of my ecstasy. The flames are licking everything in the room, burning bedding and curtains. There's ash in the air and smoke all around. Grey's still holding onto me, looking just as amazed as I am. We should be panicking but, for some reason, we just look around in awe. This fire is different than with Shax. It's almost like Shax's fire was controlling mine. This is all me.

That's when the pain starts, so intense that I can't breathe. The same seems to happen to Grey because he drops to his knees. I lose my grip on him as he goes down, but I recover just in time. The need to protect him overtakes me, and I know if I'm not touching him, the flames will eat him alive. I can't see a way out of this. The smoke is getting so thick that I begin to feel it in my nostrils. He tries to pull away, but my strength is too great for him. I crash my mouth to his on instinct as I try to call out to Cass and Shax. There's no getting through, they can't hear me, so I do the only thing I can think of –- I share my magic with him. It's completely insane, but my gut is telling me this is the only way he'll survive.

I collect it at my center and breathe it into his mouth. It's like the purple tendrils of energy I shared with Red. It seems infinite, but I know if I give him too much he will die. It's as if my magic is telling me how much to give him. As soon as I am finished, we both scream in agony, again. My plan is backfiring as I can feel the flames starting to overtake me. They are all over us in an instant. My skin feels like its peeling off. The heat is so intense, I feel as if I may be melting. The only thing I can do is hold on to Grey. I see him through the flames and look into his face. This is the last moments for us, and I want to see him before I go. He must have the same feelings because he grabs both sides of my face and pulls me back into our kiss. Tears stream down my face and get evaporated by the heat. There's so much pain.

Our kiss is one for the ages, making all my others seems unimportant. I put everything I have into the kiss. All of my regrets, fears, hope, and love. I pull him in closer so that we can be consumed together. Just as I know this should be it, the flames die out. Every one of them vanishes without a trace. I stare into Grey's beautiful unmarred face. There are no burns and no scars. I look down at my body and see the same.

Then it hits us again. This time it's pure agony. It makes me curl into myself, losing my hold on Grey. I crumble to the floor and try to ride out whatever this is. My back is on fire again, but it isn't the fire that just happened. It's burning and stretching. I don't know what is happening, but Grey is feeling it too. I hear voices in the distance, and the door is being pushed open. I hear Cass's voice and Shax is behind him. Something must be blocking the door.

Grey takes my hand in his and lets out a guttural scream. I'm not far behind him with my own torture on my lips. Then I feel it. My skin ripping from my body. The muscles and bones are contracting, and tearing can be heard around the room. I bring my gaze up and find Grey hunched over breathing heavily. "What the fuck is happening, Azra?" he asks, in between screams.

I want to answer him, but I can't. My head is bowed in agony. Just when I think I will die, a huge pop sounds. The pain is released, but it is replaced by an intense pressure. I look up in time to see Grey scream, clench his fists, and rise up on his knees bowing his back. Beautiful pearl-white wings sprout from either side of his back. I don't have enough time to think about it before I'm mirroring his actions. I can tell by his face that it's happened to me also.

The door bursts in. My mates and Red pile in. They wear looks of pure confusion on their faces. Bouncing back and forth between the both of us, I'm just as bewildered. What the fuck just happened?

6

THE FALLOUT

"*A*s I said before, I don't know what happened, Cass," I yell at him. We have been in this round-about questioning for at least a half hour. My body hurts, and these fucking wings are heavy. I just want to go to sleep, and these two idiots are just rehashing the whole thing over and over. I look over at Grey, and he is just staring out the window, not even moving or saying anything. I think he's in shock.

"Azra, we aren't trying to make this difficult. I can feel that you want to go to sleep, but we need to come up with a good reason why you have fucking wings and Greyson is now a goddamn Fae," he yells back. I don't know if it is the fact that I slept with Grey, or the fact that I turned him, that's bothering him more.

"Why do we need a reason at all? I don't see how this is anyone's business," I tell him. I'm hoping he takes this as the cop-out it is and lets me go rest.

"It's the Queen's business. Once she gets wind of your wings and what you can do, your agreement and your time here are over. This just fucked us big time," Shax says. His eyes are hard, but it's not for me. He's chosen a side. I can feel anger and fear from him, and there's something else too; protection maybe?

"Why would it matter to the Queen if I have wings? She can't use them," I ask. I tried to flap them before, and they won't move. I have paralyzed wings. But I need to know what would happen if the Queen finds out. We've already escaped one monarch, and we might have to do it again.

"Azra, no Fae has had wings in centuries. Your wings mean everything. They show the strength you have. They're going to change the way she looks at you. Your powers just increased tenfold, and you'll be unstoppable once we figure this all out and train you. She's going to use you, just like Michael wanted to. You created a fucking Fae with his own wings! Even you have to know that's special," Shax exclaims. He looks so worried.

"So, we run again," I say with a shrug. I look around the room at them and decide I might as well lay everything out while we are here. This will cause more tension, but it has to be said. "There's no good way to tell you all this, but here goes. I'm not picking a side. I'm not giving the King or the Queen access to that much power—ever. They're both a bunch of dicks, and I don't feel like Earth should be controlled by anyone. If I'm being honest, I don't think the Fae belong on Earth."

The silence in the room is deafening. No one person makes a sound. Grey even turns from his chair to look at me. I see for the first time something other than disgust—it's pride. He agrees with me. One down, two to go. I look up at my Light and Dark. They're so amazing and mean so much to me, but I won't have humanity trapped like this ever again. The Fae have their world, and I'm going to make sure they stay in it. I'll close the portals for good. Make sure no one can get in or out, and then I'll change the way things are done here. It's time to shake things up a bit. Now, I just have to get my mates on board.

"Tell me what you two are thinking," I ask them. Shax reacts first, which surprises me. I thought he would be the one to shut me down since he's been stuck here his whole life.

"I support you in what you choose, mate. I'm not going to lie to you and say that you'll be popular among the Fae, but if you do it right and you make certain arrangements, then I think we can have the backing of the people. She may be my mother, but she's a Queen first, and when Lucifer makes her mind up about something, she doesn't back down. It will be a fight, another side to this war, but I'll be at your side the whole time," he declares. I didn't think love could blossom this quickly, but I'm finding Shax has stolen a piece of my heart.

"Did you just say your mother is Lucifer? Like the Archangel who fell from Heaven?" Grey asks. He seems a bit stunned by this proclamation. I'm not surprised. Of course, she's Lucifer.

"Those stories are fictitious. Michael likes to make drama and misconstrue what is believed to be fact so that he will look better amongst his followers. There is no Heaven or Hell, there are only different realms. In this case, Earth and Faerie," Shax explains. Gods, Michael is a fucking prick.

"I would like to say something. Azra, you know that I'm devoted to you, but I feel you may be striving for the impossible. Think about this for a moment. You're changing the lives of millions of Fae. You're taking away something that most Fae dream about, living on Earth. I don't think it is wise to forge down this path. Let's make an alliance with the Dark so that we can destroy Michael," Cass responds.

"You have got to be shitting me! You want to take sides with the psycho Queen? What's wrong with you?" Grey yells. He hasn't lost his anger, even though he is now technically Fae.

"We have to play this smart. There's four of us in this room and millions of Fae on Earth and Faerie. Those odds are impossible. I want us to live, not meet our demise because we didn't think it through," Cass answers. The more he talks, the more I feel crushed.

"The whole point is to change things, not make them the same with a different person at the top. If you can't see that, then I don't know why you're here," Grey counters. His chest is heaving, and I can see he's having as hard of a time as I am with controlling his wings.

"You have no idea what you are suggesting. Azra, we can't do this. It's not something that can be accomplished. I'm sorry, but we need to stay safe," Cass says, looking at me with sadness in his eyes.

My heart drops into my stomach. He doesn't believe in me. He doesn't think I can do it. I feel the first tear fall as I get up from my chair. My wings are so heavy behind me that I walk hunched over. I try to straighten my back and pull them up, but they just fall down to the floor again. I find a bedroom to crash in and lock the door. I don't want to be near any of them right now. I just want to sleep and forget that Cass broke me a little.

Greyson

*S*he turned me into the thing I hate the most. My wings feel heavy behind me as I watch her walk into the bedroom. Cass was a dick, as usual, and doesn't think before he opens his fucking Fae mouth.

"You're a dick, you know that?" I say, looking at him with the disgust he deserves. Azra deserves to have us all on the same side. She doesn't need this asshole making it difficult for her.

"Just because you've been a Fae for ten minutes doesn't mean you can speak to me that way," he replies. I laugh in his face and turn back to look out the window.

"You aren't a prince here, Cassiel, so if I were you, I'd come down from that high horse you love so much," I say.

He doesn't reply but goes and sits in the lounge area. It's just as well because I feel like my body is still on fire. The transition was horrible. I felt like every cell in my body was being ripped open and sewn back together again with a rusty needle. And when the wings popped out, gods I thought I was dying.

My identity is torn. As a human, I had a purpose. I knew who to hate, and who to side with. The Fae took everything from me—my home and my freedom. They tortured me when I didn't listen, and threatened Logan when I wouldn't comply. My soul was in tatters, and then this girl. This girl walked into a bar. It sounds like a bad joke, but she's turned everything upside down.

I exhale the breath I was holding and try to focus on the world around me. The Dark isn't so different from the Light, although I feel a bit safer here. Logan seems to be adjusting and finding friends. He looked happy for the first time since we got caught up in this mess.

I snuck out before and went to see this Anna. The rec

center is every kid's dream. Sports courts, toys, electronics, or what I think would be electronics here, and then there were the other kids. They were laughing and smiling. I didn't approach Logan, because he was...smiling. It broke my heart a little that it took years for him to be this happy again.

Anna seemed nice enough. I feel bad for threatening her, but Logan is all I have left. Well, he was, until Azra. Even though I hate him being away from me, it's what's best. How can I drag a kid into this war? He's too little, too precious to be subjected to the violence ahead. Anna is safe. She has other children to watch out for. She's trained in defense, and I can see the fire in her eyes and the passion she has in protecting these children. I doubt myself every day, wondering if I'm doing the right thing by him. It was thrust onto me when our mother died, the responsibility of raising a child by myself. Gods, it gets me so angry when I think about the mess I put him through.

"Are you idiots done arguing? I can't listen to this shit anymore. You do realize that nothing you say or do is going to change her mind, so either get with us or get the fuck out, Cass. You're hurting her by being such a dick," I say, looking at these two morons.

"You should talk! All you do is run around angry at the world. Starting trouble, and making everyone you meet feel like shit," he replies, projecting his feelings onto me.

"Oh, fuck you, prince. I have a right to be angry. Your father imprisoned us. Made me hunt for him. Took away my freedom. Next time you want to come at me with your fucking pity party you better be prepared for battle," I yell, walking away from these dicks. I need to leave before I fucking crush him.

7

GATHERING COURAGE

$\mathcal{I}$ wake up to a dark room. The curtains are drawn open, and I can see the stars in the sky. The air blowing in from the window caresses my skin, causing goosebumps all over my arms. Getting out of bed, I feel a lightness that I didn't have when I went to sleep. Looking over my shoulder I see that my wings are no longer there. This may buy us some time to find another place to go. Whatever made them go away, I am grateful. Even though it would've been really cool to learn to fly.

The bathroom is calling my name. I quickly do my business and wash up before I make my way into the lounge. The smell of smoke and burnt furniture is still in the air. The guys are sitting all around. Grey is near the window looking as pensive as always. Shax and Cass are sitting rather close on the couch. There's a bond forming there, and I smile to myself. Logan is back, and when he sees me, he rushes right over.

"Az, I was so worried. What happened? You gave Greyson wings? How did you do that? Is he not human anymore? Do we have to leave now? I made a few friends today. They are great, but I understand if we have to go," he rushes out. This kid has so much energy.

"One thing at a time. Ok?" I ask. He nods his head, placing his hand in mine, and leads me over to the couch. I give everyone else a small smile and sit down. Turning to Logan, I start to explain what happened. "Grey and I got into some trouble. My powers set the room on fire, and in order to save him, I had to share some of my energy with him. That's when we both got wings, and he turned into a Fae. I don't know how I did it, but I guess that's one of my abilities now. We aren't sure."

His eyes are as wide as saucers. He looks so amazed right now. "Could you make me Fae? I don't want to be the only human," he says, with childlike innocence. He doesn't realize what it means to turn a human. Hell, I'm not even sure I understand the full scope of what we did.

"No, she can't," Grey yells. "You will not be going through all that, EVER!" He's a bit harsh, but I understand what he is trying to say. It was so painful for both of us.

"But I...," Logan stutters. He can't even get out what he's going to say because Grey cuts him off. He has tears in his eyes from being rejected. He wants to feel included, and Grey isn't taking his feelings into consideration.

"Maybe you should explain why, Grey. He's not going to understand otherwise," I suggest. It dawns on him then, and he takes a deep breath in.

"I can't have you go through all that pain, just so you can be like us. It was torture, kid. I felt like my whole body was burning alive. There's no way I would ever put you through that," he says a little calmer. He comes to kneel down by Logan, and for the first time, I notice he doesn't have wings either.

"Where did your wings go? Where did mine go?" I ask, looking toward Cass or Shax to explain.

"We think your wings respond to the fight or flight response. I did some research on Fae wings, and there's lore that they only come out in times of need or distress. We're lucky that little myth is true," Cass explains. I'm still fucking pissed at him, so I just give him a small smile and turn toward Grey.

"I am not sorry for what I did. I didn't know what would happen, but I couldn't see you die," I plead, asking for forgiveness. My face is awash with anguish, and I feel the tears start to form. They drip slowly down my face, and I go to wipe them away, but Grey stops me. He puts both hands in mine.

"You saved my life. That's more than anything these dicks would've done. In my mind, Fae are all the same. Selfish, ignorant, pieces of shit who could care less about the others around them. What they did to me, what they did to us, I can't forgive, but it's time that I start separating you from them. Be patient with me. It's not something that's going to happen overnight, but I'm going to try. *Mate,*" he projects the last part in my thoughts.

Holy shit! We're mates. He must see the look of shock on my face. I hadn't realized it with all that was going on, and how shitty I felt after what happened. Now that I'm checking in on myself, I can feel him there. A pulse of energy in my chest right beside Cass and Shax.

We can't keep this from them. They will start to sense you soon. Cass didn't take long to realize Shax was part of the bond.

Not now. Soon. I just can't deal with another fight at this moment. You should've heard these two idiots while you were asleep. A grin comes over his face as he continues to stare into my eyes.

"What are the two of you looking at?" Logan asks, pulling us away from our connection.

"Nothing, sport," Grey says to him. "You never told us about your time at the rec center. Did you make friends? What was it like?"

"There were lots of kids there. Some were bullies, but I found these two guys my age and they were really cool. Their names were weird, so I just called them Mike and John. We played a game that is sort of like basketball, but the net moves and you can only dribble a certain amount of times before you either shoot or pass. It was really fun," he says, looking at Grey like he hangs the stars.

"That sounds really fun. I think tomorrow I'm going to come with you and meet these friends. What do you think?" Grey responds with a smile.

"Yeah, that's cool. It beats having to do all those chores. I like it there. Anna is nice, and she said I can start lessons with the other kids. I know I'm going to be behind, but that's ok. I know I can learn fast," he says. His energy is projecting his nerves, but he wants Grey's approval.

"Why would you have to learn fast and not be on the same level as kids your age?" I ask him. He's smart. I wouldn't think he would be behind. Maybe he has a learning disability?

"I stopped going to school when we went to the Light. They don't send the human kids to learn. We weren't allowed in the same areas as the Fae kids," Logan tells me.

"They didn't allow you to go to school?" I ask. I'm already unstable with my emotions, which causes my control to start to slip. I feel like my body is heating up. I need to get out of here before I light something else on fire or electrocute someone. Turning toward the door, I quickly walk out. Behind me I hear footsteps, but I don't look back. I don't need to. I already knew Cass was going to follow me, but he stays two steps behind me. Smart Fae.

I somehow come to a set of doors that look like they lead outside. I open one up and push through. Walking out into a garden of some sort, I see benches and trees all around. There are wildflowers all over, and the air is fragrant with lavender. I stroll to the middle and lay down in the grass. The night sky is similar to ours, except it has a more purple tint to it. It almost looks like twilight is permanent here. There are millions of stars, but two moons. One looks further away than the other. I take a deep breath and try to calm down. There's so much hurt and pain rolling around inside of me. I just don't understand how Cass can try to convince me we should leave things as they are. Look at Logan. He's one of the main reasons why there needs to be change.

"Can I lay with you?" he asks, in a quiet tone. He knows he fucked up. I can feel the guilt and sadness coming off of him in waves.

"Sure, there is plenty of room," I tell him. I look up into his face and see the kind man I fell for. He's so stuck on being a Fae, he forgets that I'm here to make things different. I guess when you've lived over 500 years without change, some things aren't going to come easy.

"Azra, I'm sorry. What I said before, I was scared. I just don't see how we can come out of this on top. You're proposing changing thousands of years' worth of tradition, and you're expecting both sides to agree. You have a better chance of my father giving up his crown than you have of all the Fae agreeing to this," he confesses. He's worried. I get it. I am too.

"What makes you think they have a choice, Cass? I'm not doing this for them. I'm not doing this so one group comes out on top of the other. I'm doing this so shit like what's happened to Logan never happens again. Don't you see the filth and perverted mess your father has made? He created a system where using humans was okay. Taking them from their homes or having them born in captivity to serve him was acceptable. This is not something that's going to ever happen again for as long as I am alive. And the Queen, while she doesn't use humans as he does, and most are treated well, she doesn't treat them as equals. I can't in good conscience let a race of beings be bullied and tortured by another. I won't have it, and if you love me the way you say you do, well then you better get on board quick."

"I haven't told you I love you yet," he responds with a smile. My cheeks turn a wonderful shade of pink, and I quickly glance away. Fuck, I can't believe I said that.

He kneels on the grass beside me and gets in my face. "Look at me," he demands. "I wanted to say it for the first time, but since you took that little bit away from me, I'll say it out loud now. Azrael the Changer, I love you with all of the recesses of my being. I'm completely enamored by your beauty and grace. The way you care for people, even those of us that don't deserve it, just alludes to the wonderful person you are. I fell in love with you from our first meeting, and I want to love you for all the days that I have left."

He closes the rest of the distance and kisses me softly on the mouth, projecting all his emotions into our kiss. He lets me know how sorry he is and makes me understand he was just scared. I deepen it and grab a hold of his hair. I drag him down on top of me in the grass and moan sweet pleasures into his mouth. That's when it happens—the ground begins to shake.

8

CASTLES AND DRAGONS

*W*e quickly get up off the ground and grab onto each other. All of the trees in the garden are groaning with the movements of their roots, and the castle walls look like they could give in at any moment. There's a strange feeling in the air, almost like something is attacking the castle. I start to run toward the doors, Cass is right behind me.

"Wait! What if we go in there and it crumbles around us? You're too important to lose," he says in a worried tone. His eyes look wild, and I can sense his fear.

"My mates are in there! Logan is in there! I can't just do nothing," I shout while turning around and coming to a stop at the entrance. The entire way is blocked. There's stone everywhere, and we wouldn't be able to get through anyway.

Sensing a commotion on the other side of the garden, I take off for the gate. I hop over it with a speed that I never knew I had. My wings are out and helping push me forward. Fuck, I'll worry about that later. I need to get to my guys.

Cass jumps easily down after me, and we take off toward the chaos. I'm in awe of the sight in front of me. A dragon is wreaking havoc in front of the castle. He is massive, the size of a fucking building, stomping his feet and roaring fire. Shax and Grey are standing toe to toe with this thing. Grey is holding up his hands, and a shield is being projected from them. His wings are out as well, which is an indication of how much shit we are in.

Shax is throwing fireballs around the shield, hitting the dragon in the side. It doesn't seem to have much of an effect though. The Queen is in the distance, standing and watching this whole display. She has a sick grin on her face like she knows exactly what is going to happen. I can feel her sinister energy from here, and it tells me she has something to do with this. She's viewing the scene like she's at a play. If she wants a fucking show, then that's what she is going to get.

I pull my blade from my scabbard, and it ignites with my fire. The heat and electricity come to the surface, combining as one. Lightning crackles down the blade as I approach the dragon. He's so fucking big. I have no idea what I'm going to do, especially since I have never wielded a sword before. I'm just an equestrian show jumper from New York. They don't teach us how to fight dragons in the real world.

Grey looks over at me, and I can see the fear on his face. *Don't you fucking come over here. Get back inside. I need you safe.* He projects in my mind.

I smirk at him. *Yeah, I'm going to just stand here and let you guys have all the fun.* I clamp down the bond so he can't argue with me. I'm scared out of my mind, but I won't let it hold me back from what I need to do. Protecting my mates, and Logan, is all that matters.

Stretching the wings on my back, I give them a little flutter. It seems like they will hold me, so I try and fly up. I get about 2 feet off the ground before falling back to my feet. I try again, but it doesn't work. Cass is running to meet the guys, wildly shooting lighting at the dragon. It penetrates his thick hide seeming to hurt him at least a little bit. The dragon winces at the shock, and his attention turns full on to Cass. I have to do something. I begin to run, pumping my arms as I go, then launch myself up in the air and flap my wings. I get a good enough height and launch myself at the dragon. I manage to land on his foot. Doing the only thing I can think of, I stab down. The combination of the lightning and the fire create a crack in its skin that soon spreads up its leg. It takes only a second to ignite. The dragon roars in pain, as the fire consumes him. He bucks and tries to get me off.

I pull the sword out and jump, using my wings to guide me down in a not so graceful movement. The ground rushes up to meet me, and I slam into it with a painful smack as my shoulder takes the brunt of the fall. My wings crush under me, and I tumble ass over head across the grass. Coming to a stop, I stare straight into the eyes of the biggest wolf I have ever seen. Its yellow eyes stare into mine. It has a fluffy black coat and a white marking on its chest. Its lips are pulled back, with teeth bared. They are huge, as long as my pinkie. It gets right in my face, and some drool drips down onto my cheek. I cringe back and close my eyes. Is this another monster brought out by the Queen? I need to get back to my guys. I feel its warm breath on my face and the huff of its breath. It inhales and takes a nice whiff of my scent. I slowly try to reach my sword, that has landed next to me. My hands almost come into contact when it lets out a growl and stomps a foot down on my arm. Claws dig into my arm, and I scream out in pain. I can smell my own blood dripping from my arm. Too quickly, I feel my body run cold with chills.

A huge shadow comes from above the wolf, and suddenly it's no longer on me. I quickly jump up and do a crab walk, backing away from the new fight in front of me. Red is here, in all his Arion glory. His face has changed into that of a predator. His fangs are distended, and the veins under his eyes are so prominent. He raises his hooves and kicks the wolf in the chest as it jumps up to meet him. A whimper breaks from its lips, and my Arion neighs in challenge. The wolf backs up, clearly injured. Red is pissed. I can feel it in my chest. His eyes start to glow a pure silver as his nostrils flare. Heat starts to glow in his chest, and before I can guess what is going to happen, fire comes shooting out of his mouth. The wolf has no chance. It isn't quick enough. The smell of burnt meat and howls fills the air. I can't do anything but stare.

Red trots up to me. "Are you alright?" he asks me. He is out of breath, and smoke is coming from his mouth.

"I'm fine. Where the hell did you get fire from? Are you like a vampire dragon Arion now?" I ask, getting up to see the destruction around me. The guys are still fighting the dragon. Even with one disabled leg, it's still causing major havoc.

"I'm none of those things, and it's insulting you think so. The fire is from you. It's a good thing, too, because that wolf wasn't normal. Now get on." I waste no time jumping onto Reds back. We take off to help the guys.

"Get me to the other foot. I need to disable it somehow," I say, squeezing my thighs a bit tighter and folding my wings in. The last thing I need is to fall off.

"You're going to have to get up on its back. You need to stab it in between the shoulder blades where the wings meet. It will change back to human form after that," he explains.

"How the fuck am I going to get up there? It's like a million feet!" I yell. There is no way I can do that.

"You fly. Use your power. You're stronger now, you got this!" he yells back, picking up speed. He is racing so fast, and my wings lift off my back from the air rushing by. I'm terrified they are going to pull me off Red, but I'm too much in fight mode to figure out how to get rid of them.

"What are you? A fucking motivational poster? There's no way I can get up there." I am so nervous. If I'm the only one that can wield the sword, we are all going to die.

Suddenly, I hear a flap of wings next to me. Grey is flying next to us, keeping up with Reds speed. How the hell is he doing that? *What are you doing? I told you to get inside*, he tells me telepathically.

I'm going to try to save your ass. I just have to jump on the dragon's foot, climb up his body, and stab it between the wings. No big deal. I got this! I project back. Maybe if I say it confidently, I can believe it.

Before I can attempt it, Grey flies over me and grabs the Changer sword. I freeze time when I see him take it, but it does nothing to the four of us. Everyone else stops around us except for my mates, and Red. I scream out. He's going to burn up! No one can touch the sword! "GREY" I shout. I can hear my pulse pounding in my ears. I look up, twisting around trying to find him, but he's already speeding toward the dragon, and he's not burning up. What the fuck? I thought no one could touch the sword.

Grey lands gracefully on the dragon's back and stabs down with the sword. A shockwave ripples out from the impact, and I lose control of the time stop. Grey is thrown off the dragon as everything starts right back up again. The dragon's roars are so loud I feel a trickle of blood come out of my ears. Red pulls himself back and keeps us a safe distance from the dragon. He is wobbling on all four legs and trying to get the sword out of his back. The hilt of the sword is glowing its brilliant purple, and I see everyone shielding their eyes, except Grey. He's fine, just like I am. The dragon finally falls in a heap on the grass. He's still breathing, but you can see the pain he is in. I nudge Red to go closer. I need my sword. We get only a couple of feet before a large shimmer comes over the dragon and his huge form shrinks down to a Fae.

I hop off of Red and run over to get my sword. The guy is naked and lying in the dirt on his stomach. His hair is matted, and the color of his skin has a grey sheen to it. He's groaning and breathing heavily. My sword is stuck between his shoulder blades just as it was with the dragon. I approach him slowly and put my hands on the hilt of the sword. With one good tug, the sword comes out with a sickening pop. The man yells out in pain as I back away.

"Azra, are you alright?" Shax says as he and Cass run over. He's bloody and has a gash on his head. Cass looks like he's about to keel over, but they are both alive, and my heart absolutely soars. I run and embrace Shax first and pull him into me. His huge arms go around me, and my soul sings. I feel Cass come up to us, and I break away from Shax to pull him into the hug. I don't care if they don't want to hug me together, I need this. I need to feel both of them on my skin, which makes me think of other things, so I quickly pull away.

"I'm fine, I didn't get hurt at all. Where is Grey?" I ask, turning my body in a circle, but I can't find him.

"He went into the castle to get Logan. The boy got separated from us when the dragon attacked. I told him to go find Anna, but it's unclear if he made it to her in time," Shax explains. There is a look of worry on his face, and it makes me very worried to think about something happening to Logan.

The dragon man begins to stir, and that throws both guys into action. Shax lights fire in his hand, and Cass is standing next to him with his lightning. They look quite the pair, one dark, and the other light. Two sexy as sin Fae who are all mine. I put my sword in the scabbard and look down at the dragon man. He rolls over onto his back, and I hear an intake of breath. I look up and see the shocked look on Cass's face. He knows this man, but how?

"Cass, do you know who this is?" I ask, with a nervousness that I didn't have before. It can't be good if Cass knows this guy. He's never been to Faerie. That could only mean one thing, Michael knows we are here, and he sent someone for us.

"That's Emanuel. He's my father's assassin. I didn't know he was a dragon shifter. I guess without the magic of Faerie he couldn't shift. But if he's here..." Cass trails off. We all know what this means...time has run out.

9

FINDING ANOTHER FRIEND

*T*he Queen is in a fit of rage. There's fire in her eyes, and the air is thick with her magic. We're summoned to what is left of the throne room. Seeing her sitting on her throne tapping her fingers on the arm of the chair, my body fills with dread. Her hair is swept up by an imaginary breeze, and the energy that's pulsing off of her is making me cringe. She's going to lose it soon.

"Azra, you have disappointed me. I don't take kindly to Fae who hide things from me. There is only so much I will forgive, Changer," she says with a sneer. I need to try to talk her down from hurting one of us. I can feel the cold rush of fear creep down my body as I see the way she's looking at Grey. Our wings are out, his white and glimmering, and mine so black they are purple. She wants to pluck them off, she's so jealous. Her energy changes from the overpowering pulse of dark to a slick oily substance that makes my skin crawl. She needs to stop fucking looking at my mate.

"This just happened, before the dragon attack. They burst forth after we were mated. It wasn't planned," I say in my best boss voice. Just because I am quivering on the inside doesn't mean she needs to hear it in my tone. I can feel the shock through the bond, and then the anger. Shax and Cass are not happy I kept this from them.

"My, my, aren't we quite the collector. Three mates, and one is not so human. I wonder what else you are capable of?" she says, cold-heartedly. I feel like a science experiment. She's analyzing the possibilities of all I can do. I realize at this moment we need to get out of here, now more than ever. It's just like in the Light. Her hunger stems from power, and right now, she's starving. I can't let her get anywhere near me or the guys.

"Mother, we apologize for the lateness of us discussing this with you, but there was a dragon in front of the palace. A dragon shifter that Prince Cassiel has identified as the King's number one assassin," Shax says in a sarcastic tone. I think he might be the only one who can get away with it.

Or maybe not. The energy around her grows to a point where her eyes start to glow purple, and her skin starts to shine. She rises out of her chair and stalks over to us. She gets right in her son's face. I'm so fucking petrified of what she's going to do. My body starts to heat up, and I gather my fire right underneath my skin. She glances at me and smirks.

"Son, just because this girl is your mate, don't think for one second I won't end the rest of you and keep her imprisoned. I brought you into this world in a fury of fire and brimstone. Your life can be ended the same way. Do. Not. Test. Me." She spits out. Her whole body is shaking. I can see her hands clenching in and out trying to remain in control. It's taking everything inside her to keep from killing us.

At that moment a maid enters the room with a tray of drinks, balancing it as she walks. She looks scared as hell, and I don't blame her. The energy pulse in here would make any human run away. She makes a scuffling noise with her shoes. They squeak along the tile as she approaches us. The drinks slosh on the tray, and a little spills. She curses under her breath, and before I can blink, she's on fire and screaming. Her body ignites, and the hot flames fan our faces as we look on in horror at what just happened. I'm so stunned that I have no words. I thought Michael was an evil dictator, but this woman—she is fucking demented.

A shudder of relief comes over the Queen, and she closes her eyes and takes a deep breath. She expelled her energy, and it felt good. Her joy in killing that maid is quite evident. She turns to me as she opens her eyes, and stares deeply into mine. "You will obey. I will not say this again. Gather your things. We leave in thirty minutes for the summer palace," she says as she dismisses us, walking back to her throne and sitting down. She stares straight at us as we leave. I can't move my feet fast enough.

As soon as we are in the hallway, the screaming ensues. Cass and Shax are yelling at me, and Grey is yelling at them. I ignore all of them and keep walking. I need to figure out how the hell we are going to get out of this. We reach the floor where our rooms are, and I walk straight in. The room is a mess. Things are thrown all over, and it still smells like fire in here. Since I don't really have anything with me, I grab a few outfits that were given to me here and pack them in a bag. The guys are still arguing when I come back into the lounge. The argument is getting so heated that I see Grey start to pulse with energy. Shax has a ball of flames, and Cass is crackling with lightning.

"ENOUGH!" I yell with the full force of my power. I'm trembling from my anger. I need to reign this in before I destroy something. They all stop to stare at me. I must look fierce because they shut up immediately. "You all are my mates. I don't care if you didn't know each other before. I don't care if you hated each other. I do care about the future of this relationship. I didn't choose this, but here we are, together. There's a bond with each of you inside me that I can feel pulsing with my heartbeat. The four of us in this room, are the only ones who can stop this war. We're the only ones who can take down Michael and squash this idea of conquest from Lucifer's head. I need you all with me, working together. I'm leaving now. You best fix this before I get back!"

I hike my bag around my shoulders and make my way out of the room. Going out into the garden again, I head for the tree line. It's quieter here, as everyone is working at the front of the castle. The trees are bent in weird angles, and the flower beds are crushed. There is a crack in one of the fountains, and water is running everywhere. It's going to take a lot to get this all back together again.

I don't know how long I walk for, but I come upon a lake that has a tiny waterfall flowing on the side. The trees here were not touched by the destruction. If I close my eyes, I can almost imagine this place is serene and at peace. I can imagine living here with my mates and having a home. Taking a deep breath, I look into the pool. The water is pristine, and it looks good enough to swim in. I put all my stuff down beside a rock and begin to strip out of my clothes. The air around me is chilly, and my nipples pucker in response. Without too much thought, I take a running start and jump straight in. I submerge under the water and hit the bottom. It is silent and calm down here. The sand underneath my toes is soft and grainy. There are tiny fish floating around me, curious as to what I'm doing here. I take a few seconds to just relax. I have always loved being underwater. It's like another world and, right now, an escape for my chaotic mind.

A voice whispers to me through the current of the pool. I turn this way and that, looking for the source, but when I see none, I pay attention to the words. They sound as if they are embedded in the water. They are almost a part of it.

There will be a fourth. Accept the fourth, or you will fail.

I push up from the floor and swim up to the surface. As my head breaks the water, I fill my lungs with air while pushing my hair out of my face. I turn in a circle, looking for the source of the voice, but I see nothing. There's nothing out of the ordinary. I don't feel threatened in any way, so I lean back and float. My breasts peak out of the water, as well as my toes, as my body is pushed by an invisible current around the lake. With my ears submerged, I can only hear the silence of the water and the whooshing of my heartbeat —no trace of the voice. The silence allows me to take a minute to reflect on all that has happened since we got here. I gained three mates, created a Fae, and helped defeat a dragon assassin. The Queen is on a whole other level of crazy, and I need to get us out of here, but where will we go? What are we going to do? And how the hell am I going to convince thousands of Fae to follow me and be okay with closing the portals? I let out a sigh and turn upright. I might as well collect those idiots and find a way to start a plan.

Stepping out of the water, I shake off. I don't have a towel, so I will have to do my best air dry. I wrap my hair up in a bun and start to twirl around in circles to get the water off of me. I'm about three twirls in when I notice a white blur come across my vision. I stop where I am and cast out some energy. There's a large something past the trees in the distance. My heart begins to race because there could be anything out there. I'm all alone, naked, and have no idea how to really defend myself. I have the sword and my powers, but I have never done hand to hand combat, and we all saw what a fucking mess I made out of trying to kill that dragon. I grab clean clothes from my bag and put them on at lightning speed. I'm so nervous that my wings bust out of my back, tearing the shirt I just put on. I look around and wait for the energy source to come out. Nothing.

"Whoever or whatever you are, you need to come out and stop dicking around. I've had a shit day, and I'm not in the mood for another surprise," I yell into the trees. A few birds fly up, and some smaller animals' scuffle along the ground. I feel my soul-bond with Red and put out a distress emotion so he'll know where to find me. Drawing my sword from its scabbard, I wait to see what will happen.

A few bushes rustle in the wind, and I can feel excitement in the air. Someone is getting off on making me nervous. I feel a pulse of energy, and a man walks out from behind the trees. He is tall with tan skin, almost like he spends too much time in the sun. His brown shaggy hair is loosely draped to his shoulders. He has a brilliant set of emerald eyes and cheekbones that would make any girl swoon. His energy is pulsing in time with the earth. It's almost like he is connected to it.

He stares at me for a bit, and a smile spreads across his face. I have three mates and shouldn't be thinking about this, but holy hot damn, this man is beautiful. "What do you want?" I yell over to him. He stalks closer toward me, and I grip my sword tighter. I have no idea how to use it, but I figure if it touches him, he'll turn to ash. Right?

"I saw you swimming and wanted to say hello," he counters. His voice is like a soothing balm on a sunburn. It instantly makes me think of a quiet forest and gentle breezes.

"Why? Is it weird for a girl to swim in a lake in the middle of a forest, naked?" I ask him, and instantly regret it, because it's probably the stupidest thing I have ever said.

He laughs—the way a laugh should sound, full of joy and hope. His shoulders vibrate, and I can see a dimple in his right cheek. The scruff of his beard hid it in his smile, but this laugh brought it out. I've always been a sucker for dimples.

"Yes. It is extremely weird to see a naked Changer in a scrying pool," he tells me. This just makes me more confused because one—what is a scrying pool, and two—how the hell does he know that I'm the Changer?

"Who are you? I want to know your intentions right now. I'm extremely volatile and don't have the best control over my powers. In any moment, if I get too excited, I could blow you up or maybe electrocute you. It all depends on which one comes out of my hands first. I killed a dragon today, so you should be like, super scared," I say with not much confidence.

"I mean you..." he says, just before he goes flying into a tree and is knocked to the ground by my Arion. Red advances on him looking murderous. I see Ash in the distance waiting to see if she needs to back us up. I'm starting to really like my Arion's mate.

"What is your purpose here, halfling? Do not lie to me," Red growls out. His voice is much angrier than I've heard before. Does he know this guy? He's in his human form. I still can't get over the fact that my soul-bonded Arion is a damn man. I miss his horse form.

The man sits up against the tree and spits out a little blood. His hair is disheveled, and he is holding his side. He doesn't look too hurt, but one look at Red's eyes, and his tan skin turns a milky white. He's scared of Red and, if I'm being honest, so am I. I know he won't hurt me, but he has some major intimidation skills.

"I stumbled upon her bathing in my scrying pool. I was interested in what she was doing, nothing more," the man tells Red. Red stares at him for a couple of beats and then looks over at me.

Are you ok? he projects into my head.

I nod to tell him I am. Ash comes out of the trees and stands over with me. Red leaves the man on the ground. There's something about him that I just can't place. It's like a need in my gut telling me this guy is a piece that I'm missing. I need to find out his purpose here. Why did Red call him a halfling? With a bit more courage, because now I have two badass Arions with me, I walk over to where Red is standing.

"What's your name?" I ask the man. His eyes glow a little in the light as he gets up from his seated position. He's still clutching his side, but I can see him stand taller as he speaks.

"Gunner Lokison," he says with a slight head bow. He looks back up at me, and I swear there is something here. Something important. I'm just not catching it.

"What were you doing at the pool?" My curiosity is getting the better of me. I evaluate him again and notice that he has tattoos on his forearms and peeking out from his collar. Some of them look like tribal marks, but the others are intricately detailed pictures. They're insanely beautiful.

"I was walking back to the castle when I noticed you stomping through the forest. You're very loud, so I wanted to see where you were off to. I figured I'd watch over you until you were done doing whatever you came here to do. Then you got naked and well, I couldn't miss that, now, could I," he responds with a sly smile.

"Watch your tone, halfling," Red growls at him. I can feel the waves of anger rolling off of him, and I have no idea why. This man hasn't hurt me or said anything threatening to me. Why would Red hate him so much?

"What's a halfling?" I ask to no one in particular. Red shifts on his feet, and Gunner looks like he is going to blow a gasket. I guess the term isn't a polite one.

"A halfling is a Fae born from two different species. Gunner is a demigod. Half Norse god and half Earth Fae. His father is the God of Mischief, Loki," Red tells me. Seems like they have met before.

"And you know him?" I ask Red. He gives me a somber head shake yes and takes a quick glance at Ash. She steps up to us and grabs Red's hand. This causes Gunner to flare up in anger. You can see the grass around his feet get thicker and more luscious. I can feel his magic pulsing, it's like crushed green things, and dirt. It's intoxicating. My energy jumps to his, and before I can help it, there is an energy merge in front of us. His energy is pure green, the color of shamrocks and grassy knolls. Mine comes out in a vibrate yellow this time pulsing with the light of the sun, and together they make a beautiful chartreuse. I pull my energy back as quickly as it went out. I don't think he noticed, but my energy wants some of his. We have too many fucking problems to deal with another potential mate right now. I glare over at Red because I know he saw the shift.

"Yes, I do know him, and it isn't in a good way. There is a lot to be said for a son of Loki," Red explains, trying his hardest not to punch Gunner in the face. "We need to get back. The caravan will be moving soon, and we need to ensure the Queen sees you in it. Azra, you can ride with Ash. I will take the halfling."

"He's coming with us?" I ask Red. I don't understand

why.

"Yes, I'm coming with you. The Queen has summoned me, and so I shall answer. If you're being kind enough to provide a way to get there, I'm not going to turn it down. I have been walking for miles and prefer to rest, especially since your Arion has chosen to crack my rib," Gunner says. His eyes never leave mine as he speaks. I have this extremely terrible urge to run my hands down his body and help him heal, even though I've never done that before. He cracks a smile and walks over to where Red and Ash have shifted.

He lifts himself up with a grunt and settles on Red's back. I do the same on Ash with less grunting. We trot off to the palace, and I can hear Gunner hissing in pain, as Red moves through the trees. Ash's gait is smooth. I feel like I am riding on a cloud and not a horse. Her motions are fluid, and her back is comfortable. She evenly distributes her weight. Even without a saddle under me, I hardly jostle around. It makes me wonder what she could do on a jump course. I can measure how fantastic she would be. I wonder if she would let me ride her. Is it rude to ask now that I know she's a person too? And if she is a person, which is first, the horse or the person? So many questions to ask Red.

I hear you thinking back there. He projects in my mind. *For the record, the horse is our true form, and the person is our shift. We are born walking on all fours and will die the same. Our human skins are for when we need to hunt or blend in.*

That is so freaking cool! Do you think she would ride with me on the course? You said you liked it, so she would, right? Can you talk to her for me?

I feel his laughter come through the bond. He is snorting in my mind. I didn't think I was that funny. *I'm sure if you ask her, she will oblige. Or maybe she might tell you to go fuck yourself. It could go either way.*

LEAVING THE PALACE

The palace is a flurry of activity when we arrive. At first the guys are nowhere to be seen. Fae are running all over, loading caravans and carts. All the horses and other types of livestock are out of the stables; some I'm not sure exactly what they are. The area is still destroyed with big chunks of rock littered around the lawn. Trees are uprooted, and huge footprints pit the earth. I finally locate the guys toward the front of the castle, where most of the activity is happening.

Grey notices us first. He stops tacking Hurri and turns to meet me. I jump down off of Ash and go to him. This is the first time I have seen him since I left. I do a once over visually, and then check in with him through the bond. He seems ok, just a little tired, but we all are.

"Where did you run off to?" he asks. There is confusion on his face as he sees the new guy behind me on Red. Grey's chest puffs up a bit, and I can see his jaw clench. Through the bond I pick up on some traces of nervousness as well as a bit jealous. He definitely doesn't want anyone else to touch me.

I take his hand in mine, and tug until his concentration is back on me. "I took a walk. There's a lake behind the gardens, so I went for a swim," I say, to distract him from concentrating on Gunner.

"Stay with us from now on. I don't want to lose you in this mess," he says, as he pulls his hand from mine. In a very non-Grey manner, he leans down and kisses my forehead before turning back and finishing with Hurri.

I stand there for a few seconds, stunned, before Logan crashes into me. His arms go to my waist, and I wrap myself around him. "Hey, Wolvie. What's up?" I ask. He seems nervous about something.

"Um...Azra, did you not see the huge dragon that attacked the castle? It was so mean and huge and... mean. It had fire, and people almost died. I'm glad that Anna found me right away. I was super scared, but Greyson had to leave to help. Cause he's a Fae now. He has powers and can do cool stuff. He won't show me anything, but I bet, if you ask him, he'll do it," Logan says, in a rush. When he gets excited his mouth runs a mile a minute.

"I was there. It was a scary dragon. I'm grateful that you found Anna. Your brother was the one who stopped it. Did he tell you that?" I ask.

Logan looks at me in amazement. His mouth makes an "O" shape, and I can see the wheels turning in his head. He has so many more questions, but I cut him off before he can ask. "Why don't you help out Grey tacking Hurri, and ask him all about it? It'll be good for you two to catch up." He nods his head in agreement and takes off toward his brother.

I don't stand alone for long. A presence can be felt behind me, and I look over my shoulder to find Gunner waiting patiently for me. "May I help you?" I ask him.

"Is he one of your mates?" he asks, with a curious tone. There's so much to this Fae that I want to find out about, but not yet. There are too many things going on, and I need to figure out the bigger problems first.

"Why do you care? Don't you have a Queen to grovel to?" This gets a smile out of him. He scans my face, looking for something more. He gets nothing, I shut it all down, including the energy that's pouring out of me, trying to connect to his. This damn fucking energy. It has a mind of its own.

"Quite right. I'll leave you to it then," he says as he bows and salutes. Giving me a smile, he walks away. I don't know what it is about this Fae, but I know I need to be careful.

Cass and Shax are over on the other side of Grey. If they heard or saw the new-comer, no one said anything. Storm is tacked and ready to go. There's another horse with them that is carrying the bags and supplies that we need. I drop mine off by Cass, who is stringing the rest of them up. Since Red can't shift here, it must mean we are going to ride. I walk over to Shax, and Red and Ash follow behind. He bends down and gives me a quick kiss hello on the mouth. He breathes me in, and I relish in his touch. He tries to pull away, but I wrap my arms around him and pull him closer. He smells like fireplaces and smoke. I want to curl up against him and drift off to sleep.

"Just hold me for a few seconds. We almost died, and I need a minute to be reminded that this is real and we're safe," I tell him. I'm starting to get choked up a bit. I don't often let sad emotions overtake me, but with Shax, the feeling of belonging is so overwhelming that my guard comes crashing down.

"Always. I'll always hold you when you need it. You're my mate, Azra. You don't have to ask for my comfort," he says. His arms shift across my back, and he mushes me further into his chest. I can feel the presence of my other mate; his anxiety and fear is pouring off of him. When we get settled again, there's going to be a mate meeting. I need to know where we all stand. The future is more than I want to think about, but if I don't, then who will? There's no easy answer when you have to deal with three mates. I mean, how are we going to sleep at night?

I break my hug from Shax and turn toward Cass. He's sheepishly looking at me. I walk the three steps and pull him into the same safe hug I just got from Shax. I need Cass to get over our fight and start acting stronger for all of us. He wraps his body around mine, and I feel it then. His undying love for me. It's like a punch in the gut, it's so powerful. I feel the wetness on my face before I even realize I'm crying. Looking up at him, I see the sincerity in his grey eyes. Standing on tiptoes, I place a small kiss on his lips and back away.

"What's there left to do? I'm ready to leave this place behind. If Michael is coming, we need to be prepared as much as possible," I say, trying to shake the emotion out of my voice.

"The Queen has requested that we ride with her. I suggested we ride in the back of the caravan to get you better acclimated to the people and Faerie. There's still so much you don't know, and I wanted to use this journey to show you," Shax says. There is more to it than that, but because we are surrounded by hundreds of people, he can't tell me the whole truth.

"We need to stay as far away from that nightmare as possible. This is going to keep getting worse before it gets better. I don't believe for one second that she didn't have anything to do with the dragon attack. Did you see her face when she saw my wings? That bitch is crazy, and she wants nothing more than to use us to get what she wants," Grey says. His eyes have changed color. They're bluer now more than before. He looks like a fucking rockstar with his windswept hair and those glorious white wings coming from his back. He must still be in warrior mode because they haven't popped back in. I want to run my hands down them and see if he would quiver from the excitement. I flashback to the sex we had, and it makes me wet just thinking about it. That was some good sex.

"You need to watch what you say, Greyson," Shax whispers. "She has ears everywhere, and you don't want to find out what she does to traitors."

"I think you and me both know that I'm not the same human I was two days ago. I took down a fucking dragon. I can deal with a pissed off Queen," he retorts. A cold shiver runs down my spine as I feel the fear coming off of Shax. He doesn't want us to get hurt, but Grey needs to stop acting like an ass...again.

"Let's get mounted up. We should be moving before all these people get ready. Otherwise, we are going to get stuck. I want to be able to maneuver the horses at will," Cass says, breaking up the tension. He knows we have to move past this and, hopefully, the Queen. However, figuring out how to do that is the challenge.

Red and Ash are already tacked when I turn around to look for him. Shax goes to Ash and swings up on her back. I climb up on Red and wait for him to move. All I have to do now is place my feet in the stirrups and hold on. We don't even need to communicate what the other wants anymore.

The caravan starts a slow progression, but our four horses bypass most of the crowd. The Queen is leading the way in the front, so we try to keep a leisurely pace behind her. The scenery is beautiful. So much looks like Earth, but there are differences in color and plants. The grasses here are more yellow than green. There are these giant purple flowers that spread up the trees and bloom amongst the branches. Animals scurry about, and some even I couldn't put a name to. The sun is shining high in the sky, and I notice for the first time that it must be spring or summer because the weather is warm.

"Shax, what season is it?" I ask. I've pulled Red up to meet him.

He looks over at me with his beautiful face and smiles. "It's the beginning of summer. Our warmer months just started. We're traveling south, so it will get increasingly warmer as we go. The palace is about two days' ride from here, and I believe you'll like it there. There are beaches and a lot of trails we can take the horses on. We have a huge training facility and a nice size course for you to learn how to use your powers. Hopefully, it'll be the calm before the storm, and we can get you up to speed on using your magic," he explains.

"I'm sorry, it sounded like you said train and use my powers? What exactly did you mean?" I question. He has another thing coming if he thinks I am going to do sit-ups and run miles.

He chuckles at my shocked expression. I think my eyebrows are in my hair. I don't do well with exercise unless it's on a horse. I could never get into going to the gym. It's just so boring. "You have all that raw energy, Azra. Someone has to teach you how to use it properly. You burnt down a room, turned Greyson into a Fae, and nearly got trampled by the dragon. You need to learn how to control your energy. It's the only way to defeat Michael," he says out loud. *And the only way to ensure we can free all of Earth and Faerie*, he says through our bond.

"I am just warning you now, I don't do early morning exercise. If I need to do this, then it will be around lunch. Besides, I think I might like taking the mornings off to be with one or all of my mates," I say playfully. Sending him a heated stare, I lick my lips. His reaction is almost automatic, and I can see him shift in the saddle to get more comfortable.

"I think that can be arranged. You're the Changer, after all," he replies while clearing his throat. I instantly want to jump down off Red and take him in the bushes. Hmmm, I never have had sex in the bushes; I wonder what it would be like?

Nudging Red into a little canter, I take some time and explore a bit before we need to catch up to the Queen. If I'm being honest with myself, Shax is right. I do need to work on my control. I don't know what I am doing, and I almost killed Grey. Even when I needed to, I couldn't even fly. I need to find out how to wield these powers. The Queen and King need to be stopped, and if I'm the only one that can do it, then I need to up my game.

11

SUMMER PALACE

Two days later we arrive at the summer palace. Everything is laid out similar to the Dark Court, but here everything is open and airy. There are three turrets that stand tall against the sea. The waves crash on rocks at the bottom of the cliffs, and the birds can be heard for miles around. The breeze is warm, and the sun is ever-present. It looks more like a tropical resort than a palace for the Dark Queen.

The Queen has been keeping a close eye on us these last two days. She has summoned us every night for dinner and makes sure one or two of her guards are with us at all times. She has even set a date for a ball, one month from now, so that all her loyal subjects can meet the new Changer. At this ceremony, I am to bend the knee and pledge loyalty to the Dark Court and chose her as my sovereign. After she threw this in my lap, I made sure the guys knew that before the ball, we are leaving the palace. There's no way I'll be pledging loyalty to anyone except for my mates.

Logan has traveled most of the time with Anna and the rest of the children. He found two good friends among them and has even come out of his shell a bit. Grey wanted him to stay with us, but I explained he needed to stretch his wings, and get into trouble with boys his own age. Grey responded by yelling and walking off to cool down in typical Grey fashion.

Cass and Shax have become rather friendly. They seem to like some of the same things and even got into a heated discussion about horses and which are the best breeds. Red chimed in with the obvious—Arion—and Ash backed him on that. They haven't been able to shift while they are with us, but I feel him sneaking off into the night and meeting up with her. I don't know how he did it, being away from Ash for that long. Now that I have all three men, I don't know what I'd do without them.

We're given a suite again, but this time there are four rooms instead of three. Each of the guys has their own, as do I. The first thing I do is soak in the glorious tub that is overlooking the ocean. It is placed out on the terrace, and I have the perfect view of the setting sun. Bubbles surround me, and the scent of lavender wafts from the water. It's so peaceful here that I can almost forget what we're in the middle of. I lean back and close my eyes, breathing in the scents and listening to the sounds of my environment. It doesn't take long before I am interrupted.

"How did I know I'd find you here?" Grey asks. He has a sly smile on his face as he pulls a chair from the bathroom and places it out on the terrace next to me.

"Because you felt me through the bond, smart ass," I reply. "You knew this is where I was, and you felt me relax, so of course you needed to see why I wasn't walking around like an angry toddler like some people I know."

"I don't act like an angry toddler. I'm an emotional person. I project. It's how I let it out."

"Look, Grey, you already know how I feel. You can feel it too. I just need you to stop being such a dick for once and start realizing that we're a fucking team. It isn't just you and Logan anymore. You gained three mates. We're in this together."

"You think this is easy for me. You're the one that tore everything up. You turned me into a Fae. You made me into something that I hate. All because I listened to my dick again. If it wasn't for these goddamn feelings I have, I would have left days ago." The last bit feels like a punch to the gut. Feelings? What feelings?

"You really do know how to be a charmer. You come in here and interrupt my bath-time to tell me you regret sleeping with me? I know you didn't want to get stuck in this position, but I didn't want to either. We can blame each other for hours, or you can get in this tub and run your tongue up and down my clit, and then fuck my brains out until we have to go down for dinner. Your choice."

I don't think I have ever seen Grey stunned. It looks good on him. His eyes turn into the bright blue, and I can feel the heat rolling off of him. He gets up out of his seat and removes his shirt. He throws it on top of the chair and begins to slowly unbutton his pants. His muscles are corded and tight, his skin unblemished, and he looks sexy as hell. His Adonis belt peaks out once he starts to push his pants off his hips, and I want to reach out and lick it. My clit pulses with need, and I feel myself gravitating to the edge of the tub in anticipation.

Once he's naked in front of me, I take him all in. Our first time was rushed and frantic. I can enjoy myself this time. Chills of excitement race to my core as I can't believe this fine specimen of a Fae is mine. He climbs into the tub and wastes no time in making contact with my mouth. His kiss is fierce and demanding, just like he is. There's no gentleness to it. He fights and fucks the same. I'm all too eager to find out what it will be like to fuck him for hours without setting the world on fire.

I push him back into the tub and climb on top of him. I grab his cock and stroke it up and down. His head falls back, and I watch as he relishes in my touch. "I am going to fuck all this hate out of you. When we are done, we start new and forget the rest of it," I say with a heated glare. This is the last time I will be having this conversation with him.

Licking his lips, I ask for entrance, and he opens for me. He groans, and I quicken my movements. I trail kisses down his jaw to his neck, kissing the length of it until I get to his shoulder. I bite down in a claiming move, letting him know he's mine, ours.

Hovering over his cock, I slowly lower myself over it. Gliding all the way down him, stretching to accommodate his size. I throw my head back and pause a moment before I start moving. I rock my hips up and down in slow movements, first gathering up enough juices to make it more comfortable in the water. My thrusts become hard and faster. The water is preventing me from smacking into him with the force I need.

"Get out of the tub, and sit on the chair," I demand, frustration in my voice. He complies without an argument, and we drip water all over the floor. The sudden change in temperature charges my arousal, and my nipples pucker in response. He takes a seat, and I waste no time jumping on him with the force I need. I roll my hips and find the friction my clit desires. Our wet skin makes a glorious slapping sound, and I start to build up to my orgasm.

"Fuck, Azra. This feels so good," Grey moans out. He grabs my breasts, massaging them with his rough hands.

The friction is adding to my already increasing need for a release.

He leans me back and holds around my back to support me. Leaning forward he puts my breast in his mouth and sucks.... hard. His hot breath feels glorious against my skin. I quicken my movements creating a pounding rhythm. All of these sensations are making me come undone. I arch my back more and cry out his name. My skin alights with flame, but this time it only dances along our skin. It doesn't take long for him to soak up the heat and pulse inside of me, coming with a roar.

I place my head on his shoulder and catch my breath. I can feel his heart beating in time with mine. His breathing evens out, and the fire that's still running across our skin dulls into a warm glow. "I don't think I have ever felt anything like that before. Sex with Cass and Shax is transcendent, but this, it feels otherworldly. I don't know what is happening, but we need to find someone with answers. I don't think igniting on fire every time we fuck is supposed to happen," I say into the crook of his neck. I'm still unable to move.

"Huh...I'm better than the ying-yang twins?" he responds. My heart jumps a beat hearing his playfulness. Grey is always so angry all the time that this makes my heart soar.

"From all that, you take away that you're better than Cass and Shax?" I ask, chuckling into his shoulder. He smells like sweat and soap.

"Yes, that is exactly what I'm taking away. In fact, I am going to remind those fuckers tomorrow who the best is." I lift my head to look into his eyes. I see the brightness of his blue and a bit of emotion rimmed around it. Our bond is pulsing with happiness, and I think in this moment we just may have a shot of winning this thing together.

"You're incorrigible. It's not going to win you any points if you keep taunting them. The whole reason for this fuck-fest is to prove to you that we need you with us. I need you, Grey. You're the only one besides me that knows what it's like to be trapped by them. I need you by my side." I know my voice sounds urgent and needy, but it's the truth. We need Grey. He's my mate, and I need all the help I can get.

"Azra, I'm on your side. We're going to make the Fae understand that the shit they do is not ok. We're going to liberate the humans and trap the rest of the Fae here where they belong, even if we get stuck doing it. I'll come to terms with the guys. They aren't so bad, and we have you to bond us together. Just be patient with me. I was trapped by them for so long, it's hard for me to let go," he says, with a tinge of sadness mixed in. I wrap my arms around his shoulders and pull him in for another kiss. His body responds to mine right away.

"Let's go into the bedroom, and you can prove to me all the ways that you are better than the ying-yang twins," I say while biting his bottom lip. He growls his response into my mouth. It's going to be a fun few hours.

12

REUNION

*T*onight's dinner is in the formal dining room. The staff has decorated it to match the mood of the Queen. She sits at the head of the table with all the grace and control of a true monarch. Her dress tonight is a deep plum. A tight bodice, with a full skirt and her signature slits. Bare creamy legs peek out from where she has crossed them. A crown of diamonds sits atop her head, and the remaining jaguar from our first meeting is at her side.

There are giant black and purple silks hanging from the ceilings creating an intimate dark feeling. Floral decorations are placed throughout the hall and on the main table. There must be over one hundred Fae in attendance, all in various style of dress. This party has the same feel as the one I attended in the Light; it's just a bit more sinister. There's an angry vibe in the air. One that keeps me on edge.

"Have I told you how beautiful you look tonight?" Shax whispers in my ear with a sultry tone. I have on a long black fitted dress with an exposed back. The sweetheart neckline is hidden under a sheer mesh that has rhinestones all over it. They cover my throat, making it unnecessary to wear any kind of jewelry. My hair is pulled up in an elegant twist so that my back is on display. Shax's hand is resting on the small of it, while Cass has my arm tucked in the crook of his. Grey is behind me with Logan at his side. I feel the ever-regal Changer I was born to be.

"You look just as delectable. It's taking a lot of control for me not to grab you and run into a closet somewhere," I counter. They are all dressed in matching fitted suits. They look like well-dressed bodyguards. Cass's pale hair shines in the candlelight, giving him a halo, while Shax's jet black hair fades into the night, making him look even more mysterious. The tailor had to cut slits in the jacket of Grey's suit to accommodate his wings. While mine are tucked away, his no longer fade into his back. Either he's in constant fight mode, or his wings are here to stay. Little Logan has on a mini-suit just like the guys, making him look just as adorable as ever.

"I need a drink," Grey says from behind me. He brushes past us and goes to the bar. Logan comes up behind me and grabs my hand, making Shax move to accommodate him. I can feel his nervousness in his energy.

"Don't worry, Wolvie. I'm with you the whole night. Nothing bad can happen here. We got this," I say.

"I know, Az. It's just all these Fae. They look a little weird. I feel like they are all looking at me," he confesses. His hand is gripped tightly in mine. I pull him in closer to give him a side hug and to reassure him all will be fine. I wish he wasn't even in this mess to begin with. I'd love to send him somewhere safe.

"Let's go have a seat. I think Logan will feel better with us all gathered around him," Cass says. He's ever the thoughtful gentleman. I look up at him with admiration and love. He can be so sensitive when he wants to be.

Making our way through the tables, we find that we have been assigned to sit near the Queen. Grey joins us, and we all take our seats. A bell is rung and the rest of the guests come to their seats. The servants waste no time in placing courses in front of everyone. So far, the food here has been excellent. I don't know what half of the food is, but it's probably best not to ask.

Conversation ensues around us, and I'm soon lost in the sounds of people laughing and having a good time. The energy picks up as each course is laid out. The weird vibe I was getting before heightens, and I look over at the Queen. She's looking at me with renewed interest. I just know that she has something planned.

Around the main course, the door to the dining hall opens up, and in walks Gunner. He's dressed similar to the guys, except his tie is in a green color, matching his gorgeous eyes. I get this excited feeling in my stomach, and waves of heat rush through my body. He takes the empty seat in front of me, and my energy starts going nuts. It automatically reaches for him. Immediately, I have to clamp it down before a magical show happens in the middle of dinner. Gunner's eyes widen, and I know this time he felt it. Shit!

"So glad you could join us, Gunner," the Queen says in her best conniving voice. She definitely has something planned. Her eyes look back and forth between Gunner and I. I wonder if she could feel the energy surge.

Beside me, Shax has gone stiff. His magic has come to the surface, and it's pulsing for a release. My own matches his, and I get an overwhelming sense of anger bleeding through. Looking over at him, I see his jaw is tight and hands are clenched. He looks like he is going to flip this table.

"Son, I hope you are just as happy as I am with Gunner's

return. I brought him here for your mate," says the Queen sweetly. Her smile spreads wide across her face, and this is why I have been feeling on edge. Gunner isn't wanted.

"What do you mean he's here for Azra?" growls Shax. His eyes are a blazing fire, and I know we are going to have to leave soon before something happens.

"He's to be her teacher. We need the Changer ready for battle, and if the dragon fight was anything to go by, she is not up to par. She has no idea how to wield her sword, nor use her defensive magic," the Queen explains. She looks rather smug in that chair of hers. I want to punch her in the throat. For the first time, my anger outweighs my fear for her. It may have to do with Shax feeding that anger through the bond. I glance over at Cass and Grey, and they seem to be just as pissed.

"She doesn't need him. She has Cassiel and I. We will teach her to wield her sword and her magic. The Changer sword cannot hurt her mates, Gunner will perish if he touches it, and we all know how much you wouldn't want that to happen," Shax snaps at her. I see her own anger come to the surface; her patience is going to run out soon. We really should be leaving.

I place my hand on Shax's arm and stop him from saying something stupid. "It's ok, Shax, whatever the Queen's wishes are, I will comply," I say, giving her a tight smile. My eyes give away my words, though, she can taste my lie hanging in the air.

This seems to calm Shax down a little because he relaxes his grip on the knife that he was holding. He's still glaring daggers at Gunner, but at least he isn't going to jump across the table like before. Gunner has been quiet, watching this whole interaction until now. I think he wanted to see the reactions of everyone.

"Azra, have you ever had sword training?" Gunner asks while taking a bite of his food. His energy is relaxed even though he keeps sending it out to mingle with mine. Thank gods I have so much control over hiding mine. I guess it's from so many years of keeping it a secret subconsciously, I have even more control over it now.

"No," I say, with a curt tone. "They don't have Sword Training 101 on Earth. We mostly do math and science."

"I see," he says in a condescending tone. "We will start from the beginning then. I'll be in the training room at dawn. Try not to be late."

A growl can be heard from my other side. *We need to get out of here. Make an excuse. I don't care what you say, but if I have to look at this smug bastard for one more moment I'm going to reach over the table and punch him in the mouth. No one talks to my mate like that,* Grey says in my head. It seems like the others heard it too, because before I can react, Shax is standing up.

"We're going to retire to our rooms, Mother. Thank you for dinner," Shax announces, while getting up from his chair. We all follow suit before she can say anything.

"Understandable. You want to make sure Azra has a good night sleep so she can be fit enough in the morning for all that physical activity she'll be doing," she says nonchalantly, like she's talking about the weather and not taunting her son.

It's Cass's turn to pull Shax away. The boys make for the door, and as I glance behind me, I see Gunner looking on with such longing that it breaks my heart. Shax has a lot of explaining to do.

We get back to the rooms and we each go our separate ways to get changed. I take a quick shower to rinse off the bad feelings that dinner left me with. Throwing on a pair of loose short shorts and a tank top, I wander back into the lounge and take a seat on the couches by the fire. The guys must still be getting undressed, so I'm alone for a moment. The flames are dancing in the slight breeze that's coming from the terrace. The smell of the ocean mixed with the smoke is intoxicating. I close my eyes for a moment to take in all that happened at dinner. There are so many questions that need answers. Every day here just gets worse and worse. It's like I am always being tested, and I can never pass.

"Hey, you ok?" Shax asks from behind me. His strong hands brace on my shoulders as he lowers his body down and kisses the top of my head. His scent matches the smoke in the air, and I just want to pull him down on top of me and cuddle into his neck.

"As good as can be expected. We have a lot to discuss. Where are the guys?" I ask, looking behind him to see if they have emerged from their rooms.

"While you were showering, Greyson took Logan to go stay with Anna for the night. He's worried that something might happen, and the children's wing is the safest in the palace. All Fae know children are precious and to not go anywhere near there unless they want to face the wrath of my mother," he says with a very serious tone. It brings me a bit of joy knowing that the children are taken care of here.

"And Cass?" I ask, with a concerned tone. I don't like any of the guys being away from me.

"He went to get us some food and drink. I know you didn't eat much, and I figured you'd be hungry after your shower."

"You guys think of everything. Thank you. Come sit with me while we wait for them to come back. I want to snuggle," I tell him, looking over my shoulder. He gives me a squeeze and walks around the couch. He plops down next to me, and I snuggle up to his chest. His warmth instantly comforts me, and I feel his hard body through his light shirt. I climb onto his lap and put my head in the crook of his neck. I don't think I can ever get used to the feeling of being safe and cared for by these men. I didn't know what I was missing until now.

"You keep making those little sighing noises, and I'm not going to be able to control myself much longer. It's bad enough that you keep rubbing against me when you wiggle around. Add in the noises, and you're going to have a problem on your hands," Shax says in a husky tone. I look up into his face and see the passion there. He wants me badly.

"How much time do you think we have?" I ask, trailing kisses down his neck. His head falls back, and his hands tighten on my waist.

"Maybe ten minutes," he says with a moan. I can feel his excitement underneath me. My clit pulses with the thought of riding him right on this couch.

"Well then, let's make the most of it," I say as I crawl up his lap and straddle him. I slam my lips on his and invade his mouth with my tongue in urgency. I slide my hands around his neck and start to grind on him. He lets out a low moan in pleasure as I increase my speed. The friction of material between my legs is causing me to get so wet.

His hands cup my ass, and I speed up my movements. He breaks the kiss and says, "Take your pants off. I need to fuck you." Excitement rushes through me, and I quickly comply. Hopping up, I wiggle out of the barrier we had between us as he does the same. Enthusiastically, I jump back on him and resume pressing into him. Rolling my hips in a circular motion, I watch his face as he throws his head back in ecstasy. I'm so wet that I am causing a delicious slipping motion between us. I inch myself back a bit and pull his cock free from between us. I give him a few powerful pumps and revel in his arousal for me. Leaning forward, I place him at my entrance. I brush a soft kiss on his lips as I slam down onto him. A moan escapes my lips, and I hold for a minute, relishing the feel of him inside of me. Then I begin to move.

"Gods, Azra. You feel amazing. I could fuck you forever," he whispers into my lips. He pushes my shoulders back and pulls my tank top down to expose my breasts. He wastes no time leaning down and taking one into his mouth while twirling and pinching the other. A rush of sensations roll off of me, and my fire lights us up. His fire rushes to meet mine, and a beautiful purple glow fills the room. My movements quicken as my instincts take over, and I start to pant in my efforts. My grip on his shoulders tighten. I'm close to coming.

A cool breeze comes over the room, and I look up toward the door. In the doorframe, Grey is staring at us. I hold his gaze and continue to fuck Shax with a renewed intensity. His eyes light up with heat, and the blue staring back at me is so intense that I swear I see the energy rolling off of him. He likes what he sees. Through the bond I can feel his excitement as well as his hesitancy. I don't think he is ready for a threesome. Continuing to watch Grey, I proceed to pump up and down on Shax and make him hiss out my name. Grey's hand goes to his pants, and he releases his cock for me to see. He gives it a good squeeze and begins to jerk himself up and down. My arousal increases tenfold, and I almost lose it then.

"Shax, reach down and rub my clit. I want to come all over your cock and make you call out my name," I say to the room. This gets Grey even more excited. I can see his energy start to pulse around him. He must be getting so close. Shax reaches between us, and beings to massage me. A guttural moan leaves my lips, and I cry out. I'm so close to orgasming, that I can't help but push harder and faster.

I clench around Shax, biting my lip hard enough to draw blood. My pussy pulses with the pleasure of my orgasm as Shax takes over. He lifts me up off of the couch and spins me around to face the door. Standing behind me, he wastes no time slamming into me...hard. His erratic movements have me grasping the back of the couch and my breasts swinging to the rhythm. I hear his intake of breath as he notices Grey in the doorway. He doesn't stop fucking me but asks if I'm ok through the bond. I nod my head and bring my gaze back to Grey. His hand is pumping so hard, that it almost looks painful. He's leaning on the open-door frame, and his eyes are locked onto me.

Shax is hitting all the right places, making me feel magical and otherworldly. Our flames are still mixing, and I see our energy leave us and snake out toward Grey. Once it hits him, a loud moan escapes his lips as he comes into his hand. This pushes me over the edge, and I pulse around Shax once again. My tight muscles send him into a spiral, and I milk every last drop of him. I fall forward onto the couch and try to catch my breath. That was one of the best sexual experiences of my life. I had no idea how much I would love to be watched.

Without missing a beat, Grey strolls over to me, dick still in hand, and claims my mouth. He puts it all into that kiss. I can feel his growing emotion toward me, and his acceptance of this new life. Through the bond, I can feel his anger slowly melting away, and the determination he has to make this work between us growing. I finally feel the hope I was looking for all along.

He breaks the kiss and looks into my eyes. "I'm going to take a shower. I think we all need to talk. When will Cassiel be back?" He asks.

"He should be back any minute. I agree, we all need to chat," I respond back to him. He gives me another quick peck and walks into his room, shutting the door.

"That went a lot better than I expected," Shax says from behind me. He leans over and nuzzles his face into my neck. The gesture is sweet, but it turns me on at the same time. I need to put a little space between us before I go asking for round two.

"You mean Grey catching us, or Grey watching us? 'Cause I was surprised by both. I thought for sure he'd get pissed and leave like he usually does," I confess.

"He looked like he enjoyed it, and when you sent him your energy, he looked like he *really* enjoyed it. I'm just happy that he's ok with sharing, but you guys are right, we need to have a talk. As Alpha, I need to make sure everyone knows where they stand."

"I hadn't even thought of that. What is your role, exactly, as alpha?"

"I'll explain everything when the guys come back. Why don't you jump in the shower, and we can meet out here in five? Cassiel should be back with the food by then, and we can dive into our relationship dynamics."

I nod my head in agreement and make my way to the bathroom. I run the water and quickly wash off the evidence of the delicious sex we just had. It was hot as fuck letting Grey watch us. It makes me think of all the other advantages having multiple mates can bring, like watching two of the guys embrace their inner kink. My mind wanders off, and before long I am clenching around my fingers, wishing all my dreams would come true.

When I step out into the lounge, all the guys are sitting around the table devouring the food. There are sandwiches, chips, and fruit. Pitchers of wine and water sit on the table as well. I pull up a chair and get to work on one of the sandwiches. The bread is crusty and warm, and the meats and cheeses are flavorful.

"So, did you know where you wanted to start?" I ask Shax. He's finishing up his sandwich. He wipes his mouth with the napkin and gets up to pour me a glass of wine. It's a blush color, and the aroma is rather sweet. He hands me the glass, and I take a sip, leaning back in my chair and waiting for an answer.

"I think I should explain what the roles in our relationship are since you and Greyson are both new to the Fae. Then we can all talk more about our wants and expectations," he says. His posture is relaxed, putting me at ease. His hand comes over to mine and gives it a slight squeeze.

"That sounds good. Have at it, professor," I say in a saucy voice. He gives me a look of pure heat, and I shift in my seat.

"Ok, as you know, we are all Azra's mates. We're her lifelines and protectors, as well as the source for all her energies. Her mates are designed to help her navigate through her powers, ground her when necessary, and share energies with each other. It is a mechanism that was built into the Changer's magic, so that she alone could change the fate of the Fae control. Of course, our bond includes other things such as the intimacy we feel for her and the attraction we get whenever we are around her. I'm not sure why the magic gives us that bonus, but I'm not complaining," Shax says with a smile. He reaches over and brushes a stray hair behind my ears. His affection is written all over his face, and I lean in and give him a sweet kiss on the mouth.

"What do you mean when you say, 'share energies'? I

have never heard of this," Cass asks, his intellectual side peeking through. I can feel how excited he is about learning something. It must be few and far between when something new comes along for him.

"When we all get strong enough and train hard enough, we can share each other's energies and powers. I'll be able to command lightning, and you both will be able to use my fire. I'm unsure what we'll be getting from Greyson besides that shield he can cast. His powers haven't seemed to fully manifest yet, but when they do, we can share those as well. There is only one problem—we don't have our fourth," Shax explains.

"What do you mean our fourth?" I ask with a look of concern on my face. Could this have anything to do with what the scrying pool mentioned? Gunner. A ripple of shock goes through my system as I realize this truth.

"The fourth mate. The Changer always has four. One for each of the elements. That means Greyson is either water or earth, and your fourth is the other," Shax says in an educational tone.

"You mean we get another fucking Fae prick in this bunch? You're not talking about that asshole from dinner, are you? The one that was playing footsie with Azra's magic. I was getting a headache with how much he was putting out. I was ready to reach over the table and knock him out when your mom started all that shit with the training. I figured you'd take it from there since it looked like you had a problem with him already," Grey says nonchalantly to Shax like he didn't just drop a fucking bomb.

"Playing with her magic? Azra, care to explain?" Shax asks, raising his eyebrows and giving me a shocked expression. Fuck! My palms get sweaty, and I feel the nerves crawl up my body.

"I didn't know how to tell you all. It happened when I met him in the woods when I went swimming. His magic and mine, they umm...want to join together. It kind of feels like what happened when we met, Shax. But then I shut it off somehow, and when I saw your reaction to him tonight at dinner, I knew it wasn't wise to talk about it. Red doesn't like him either," I rush out. I don't know why I feel so nervous right now. It's not like I did anything wrong. This fucker is the one everyone has the problem with.

"He's our mate," Cass says to no one in particular. He looks like he's ready to pass out. Why does everyone have a problem with this guy?

"So, what if he is? I know you guys don't like him, but why? I'm so clueless right now," I tell them.

"Gunner is the Dark Court's assassin. He's the only one the Queen trusts to do her dirty work. He has killed thousands of Fae, and not cared a single second for the lives of anyone around him. He's a prick and a fucking fake. He has no feelings, and there's no way he is our mate!" Shax yells as he slams his fist on the table. The glassware rattles with his outburst, and I reach out to hold mine still.

"Who has he killed that has you so riled up? Usually, the Fae only get excited when it affects them directly? So, *Cat,* who did he hurt?" Grey asks, with a gruff tone.

"My sister," Shax says with a rush of breath. His hands go to his head, and he pulls at his hair a little. He's hurting so much, and I can feel it through the bond.

"I thought you said she died in battle. How would the court assassin kill her?" I ask.

"Sola was killed by Gunner in battle. I didn't tell you the whole truth before because I was ashamed of my mother. Sola was the leader of the rebellion. She was trying to overthrow the Queen before it was her time to rule. Some of the Fae here want more from their ruler. They want freedom and not to be used for their resources. They want fair wages and not to have to look over their shoulder for saying or doing the wrong thing. You saw how my mother burned up that maid for no reason. She's been doing that for centuries," he says, looking a little defeated.

"Well, that's...fuck, this puts us in an impossible situation," I say.

"Yeah, you could say that. I don't know anything about your sister, but I'd fucking cut that guy's throat if he ever did something like that to Logan. I still might do it just for him looking at Azra. I don't want him in our harem," Grey says. His voice is firm, and I believe every word he says.

"We don't have a choice. If that's who the magic is calling to, we need to accept him in order to fight Michael and Lucifer. There is no other way," Cass says. He doesn't look like he's agreeing with adding Gunner in, but ever the logical one, he sees what we need to do.

I look around the room at the guys. No one's happy about this revelation. I don't know how we are going to fix it. What if the Queen knows? She's going to have an inside man in our little group if Gunner is loyal only to her. I wonder if she brought him here just for that. She must have noticed her son switched sides. We need to figure this thing out, and sooner rather than later.

"What's the plan? We need to make it seem like we don't know. If the Queen sent him as a spy, maybe we can use it to our advantage? We train, get the most out of it, and try to find a way to beat them without him. I don't like this situation either, but we need to make it look like we're doing what she says. There's too much at stake here," I say. Inside, I'm freaking out. How could my magic choose someone so horrible? It scares me that we need him, and it scares me even more that I want him.

"Agreed. Let's get some rest, and worry more about this tomorrow," Cass says. "I also would like to sleep in bed with you. I don't trust having two assassins in the castle, and not being able to protect you."

"Me too. I don't want anyone slipping through," Grey says, walking into my bedroom without waiting for permission. I follow after him without saying another word knowing both Cass and Shax will follow.

When I enter the room, Grey is already sprawled out on the bed. His wings taking up a good part of it. There really is only room for two more. I don't want to choose between them. Before I can voice my opinion, Shax offers, "I'll take the couch. You and Cassiel have the bed. We can rotate nights, or I can have a bigger bed delivered tomorrow. Your choice, Azra."

"Bigger bed, please. I want you all around me," I say quietly while crawling into bed. I roll onto my side facing Grey. He gives me a small smile and closes his eyes. His hand reaches over and grabs mine. I can feel his protectiveness, and it makes me feel safe. The bed dips behind me, and Cass nuzzles into my back. I feel the loss of Shax but know he's there if I need him. I'm happy in this moment. My heart is full, and it feels like home.

13

A TRAITOR IN OUR MIDST

The next morning, I wake to my body being on fire. Not literally, but the heat that's under these covers is intense. The two men sleeping next to me are draped all over. I can't say that I mind, but I'm sweating. Trying to shift without waking someone up, I feel a hard presence pressing on my back.

"If you don't stop wiggling around, I'm going to take you right in front of the guys," Cass whispers, in my ear. My cheeks blush pink, and my arousal peaks. I get a little too excited thinking about us all together and have to shift some more to relieve the pressure.

"I don't think that would be a bad thing, do you?" I ask with a seductive tone. Reaching around, I grab his hard cock in my hands over the tight boxers he has on. I begin to rub up and down. A moan escapes him, and it sends a thrill through me. I love having this effect on them.

He slides his hand that's already wrapped around my waist down to my core. Slipping it into my shorts, he finds my sensitive nub. I spread my legs apart and lean my head back into his chest. My pumping increases with my arousal, and we begin to move in tandem. It doesn't take me long to get to a crescendo of feelings. It comes in waves, and my pussy clenches, pulsing out my pleasure. I can feel his heavy breath on my neck, and a few pumps later he comes into my hand. We stay there for a second, basking in the glow of our morning orgasms.

"You could've asked if we wanted to join. It's unfair to have morning sex without inviting the rest of us," Shax says from the couch. His hair is all tussled, and his just woke up face is positively gorgeous. It makes me want to ask him to come up on the bed.

"If you heard us, you should have joined. We could've made this into a more wonderful morning," Cass says, with heat in his voice. Holy hotness! Now I'm officially turned back on.

"I wouldn't have minded," Grey says with his eyes closed, and his face still stuck into the pillow. Now I definitely need to take a cold shower. I get up out of the bed and run toward the bathroom as I hear sounds of laughter behind me.

I quickly shower and get ready for the day. We eat in the lounge and then walk to the training yard to get started on the day's activities. The boys have been in a protective formation since we left, with Shax in the lead and my other guys on each side. The Fae that are in the courtyards and castle grounds stare and whisper as we walk past. I don't know if it's because of our wings, mine popped out as soon as we left our rooms, or if it's because I'm walking with two of the most powerful Fae, but they all look at me with questionable expressions.

Gunner is waiting for us in a huge building that has been chosen to be my training grounds. Guards are flanking either side of the entrance, and I get the odd suspicion they aren't there for me. They are wearing official uniforms and carrying those weird amber looking guns that I saw on my first day here. The building is one big massive room with a ceiling at least thirty feet high. There are barrels of hay stacked in one corner and various weapons hung about on the walls. I see different sized swords, axes, knives, guns, and something that looks like a large mallet. Targets are stationed about in the far corner, and there's a pool of water off to the side. It all looks so utilitarian. I imagine it to be something the military would use for training.

"Good Morning, Azrael. I didn't think you'd bring your entourage with you," Gunner says, with a smirk spread across his beautiful face. His magic reaches out again with a teasing pulse, and I cut it off right away. I'm starting to get perturbed with his persistence to let our magic intertwine.

"My name is Azra, not Azrael. The guys are here for my protection, *assassin*," I say in a snarky tone. I don't want to like this guy. He killed Sola and countless other Fae. I don't even know what the story is with Red yet. My body betrays me, though, because my energy zings out to meet his of its own accord, like it can't stay away. I feel the pull right away, the desire to be close to him, and I shut it off even harder. Gods, this is getting annoying. I'm going to need to say something regardless, even though we said we wouldn't. It's too distracting. I will never be able to learn to fight.

"Dude shut the fucking energy off. We can't be in here all day with you trying to get to Azra. Either you fucking play nice, or I slam my fist into your face," Grey threatens. He looks like an avenging angel with his gleaming wings. His broad chest is puffed up in anger and his chiseled jaw set in determination. I can't believe I get to say he is my mate.

"So, you all feel it. I was wondering when you lot were

going to catch on," Gunner says with amusement. He beams a smile at me and the guys. He thinks this is hilarious.

"You'll never be her mate," Shax says with gritted teeth. He's so angry that fire forms in his hands. It doesn't seem to faze Gunner. He just continues to stare at the guys like they are discussing something mundane and not the fate of the Fae realm.

"I don't think that's for you to decide. The magic has chosen me to be her fourth. You can't defeat Michael without a fourth. It seems you are stuck with me one way or another," he counters with a smug look on his face. There's no way this is going to end well. I can sense the tensions rising with the guys.

Shax goes to take a step forward, and I reach an arm out to stop him. "Let's get started with the training. We're here at the bequest of the Queen, and we need to comply," I say to the guys. "I'm not mating with anyone else, so please keep your energy to yourself," I say to Gunner. I go further into the room and take another look around. There are mats laid out in what looks like a sparring circle, and a bunch of machines are located on one wall. They remind me of the gym equipment I would use back home.

Standing in the center of the mats, I call out to Gunner, "Let's get started, shall we?" The guys all move over to the side of the room and have a seat on the hay barrels. There's no way they will be leaving this building.

He gives the guys one final glance and comes to stand with me. He's wearing sweatpants and a tight tank top show-casing all the muscle that he has going on. His shoulders are broad, and his tattoos are on full display. I catch myself staring a little too long and quickly look up to his face. A huge smile meets me, and I know I've been caught.

"What do you know about swords or sword fighting in

general?" he asks, glancing at the Changer sword strapped to my back. Cass fit the scabbard around my wings so that I could carry it today. He says we should get a custom one made so that I can have my wings in or out without having to take it off—good for when we are in battle.

"I know that the pointy side is the one you show your opponent, and if you touch my sword, you will disintegrate into ash. Beyond that, I have nothing," I say in an honest tone.

"Well then. We have a lot of work ahead of us," he says with an exasperated sigh. I can see that he isn't too keen on wanting to work with a newbie, but it's not my fault the Queen stuck us together.

"Let's get this over with then. I don't want to be here anymore than you do."

"You're wrong there, Azra. I'd love to spend time with you, anytime, in fact."

I glance up at him and try to gauge if he's telling the truth. My magic is doing flip flops in my chest, but I just can't accept a murderer into my harem. He killed my mate's sister, and my soul bonded doesn't like him. I need to go talk to Red.

"Nope. I don't need to see you except for when it's mandatory. If the Queen didn't request this little lesson, I wouldn't even be here in the first place. Now let's get on with it."

He steps up and places an arm around my shoulder to reach for the sword. He doesn't grab it by the hilt, but rather undoes the ties that secure it to my back. Once it's free, he uses his other hand to clutch the scabbard. Both of his arms are around me now, and it's getting hard to concentrate. He smells like frost on trees, and lilacs in the spring. I find myself leaning in and taking a sniff. He chuckles at my actions, and I step back clearing my throat.

"Next time just go from behind," I say in a flustered tone. I realize how that came out when he begins to laugh straight in my face. I feel the blood rush up, and I must be a wonderful shade of pink.

"As you wish, my lady," he says, after he stops laughing his ass off. I swear I see tears glistening in his eyes. It wasn't that funny.

We practice for most of the day. He teaches me stance and balance, how to hold the sword properly, and how to block. We practice drills to get my arms accustomed to the weight of the sword, which becomes a lot heavier as the time goes on. He goes through different scenarios with me, and when I finally get one right, he declares we are done for the day. All in all, I am glad we came. Even if this guy is evil, he gave me a valuable lesson on how to stab someone properly with a sword.

Walking over to the guys, I see they are just as anxious as I am to get out of here. Grey gets up first and pulls me into a hug. He bends down and nuzzles my neck while wrapping his wings around me. We're in our own little bubble when he places a soft kiss on my mouth. "I'm glad that's over because I was going crazy standing here watching that asshole put his hands all over you. I wanted to punch something," he whispers into my mouth.

"You always want to punch something," I reply. I grab his bottom lip between my teeth and give it a tug. He lets out a hiss of pain but presses into my front more. I know if we stay together like this, we aren't going to make it out of this building. I quickly kiss his lips again, and then I back out of our little cocoon.

Shax and Cass come up to me, and each lay a kiss on my

head. We walk hand in hand, with Grey trailing behind, out of the building. The sun has almost set, and my stomach growls in response. We really did spend all day in there.

"Let's get you fed, and then I was thinking we could all go for a ride. We haven't done that since we got here, and I'd like to check on the horses. Storm isn't used to being without me for long," Cass says, looking toward the barn in the distance.

With all that has been going on, I haven't told the guys about Red and Ash. It completely slipped my mind. "Yes, let's go see the horses. I am sure Red has got a lot to say."

I glance up at Shax and give him a sly smile. I can't wait for everyone to freak out when they see Red shift for the first time. Shax returns it and gives me a quick wink before anyone notices. I stifle a chuckle and keep walking in the direction of the palace.

After having a quick meal and showering, we all head to the stables. Grey picked up Logan from Anna's and he is now talking non-stop about the sleepover he had with his new friends. You can see the light in his eyes coming back. He's starting to be the boy I knew he was this whole time. Even though we are still in major trouble, it's good to know there is one positive thing that came out of this. Logan is blossoming. I hear him rambling on to Grey as we walk.

"And then we ate these things that looked like cake, but it really wasn't. It tasted like pizza. Remember pizza, Greyson? Ugh, it was so good! I wish you guys were there. I mean, sort of. I really love you all but being with friends was really nice. If you want, next time I can bring you back some. I don't think you want to hang out with boys. Right, Az? It's ok if I just bring it back. You don't have to come," Logan says, with his vibrancy turned up to a thousand. He is such a wonderful boy.

"You're right, Logan. I don't think us grown-ups would have any fun with you guys. I think you and your friends are better off by yourselves," I reply. He looks up at me with the brightest smile.

"Thanks, Az. You're one of my favorite people," he says.

"And you're mine," I reply.

We reach the stables a few seconds later, and the smells of horses hits me instantly. To say that I am obsessed with horses is an understatement. It's what I lived and breathed for most of my life. Ever since I was a little girl, horses have always been the thing I have wanted to be surrounded by. Whether it was riding or grooming, I was happy to do it all. When I had the opportunity to show jump in the Winter Equestrian Festival two years ago, I thought I had it all.

The course was super tough that day. My horse Sharott was on edge for some reason. We walked the course together counting strides and getting ourselves used to the environment when, out of nowhere, he spooked. Full on reared up, shaking his head and backing up like he was afraid. I just took it as a freak thing and continued on with the day. When it was our turn, he took his turns beautifully, following my every move. His jumps were swift and smooth with him landing gracefully every time, and then the last jump came, and he froze in mid-air. His front legs got tangled in the top bar, and we both went flying to the side. I made the quick decision to push myself away from him. Otherwise, I would have been crushed. He broke his right front leg that day, and his owner pulled us from the competition. His leg would never heal correctly, and I was blamed for the misjudge in the jump. My luck as a professional show jumper ran out. I was done.

I shake off the bad memory and look around me. The stables are just as immaculate as I remember them. The stalls are full of different breeds of Fae horse, some looking a lot like Earth horses, and others looking nothing like them.

Walking down the halls the same as the other day, we reach the branch that houses our little herd. Storm rushes to meet us as we approach his stall. He swings his head out and throws it up in the air in greeting. He's excited to see Cass, and from the look on his face, Cass is too.

Red's stall is next to Storm's, but he isn't in it. I look over at Shax, and he gives me a shrug as if to say, 'I have no idea where he is either.' Hurri is across from the guys, and I can see that they moved Ash in next to Hurri, although her stall is empty as well. Tricky Arion shifters.

Just before I try to go looking for them, Red's energy comes out to me loud and clear. He's in the meadow behind the barn. They want to finish Shax and Ash's ritual tonight. I take in all the rest of what he has to say and then turn to the group.

"We're going for a ride, and you are all going to get to be part of a celebration," I say, with a little wink to Shax. He catches on to my meaning, and I feel a jolt of happiness from him as he smiles wide. He's excited to finish his soul-bond with Ash.

"What do you mean celebration? Is there going to be food? Cause we ate like forever ago, and I could use some more of that pizza cake," Logan asks, with hopeful eyes.

"You just ate like 25 minutes ago, Logan," Grey says in an adult tone. He's trying to be a super serious parent right now, but is failing miserably, especially when Logan turns around and gives him a huge smile.

"Twenty-five minutes is a really long time for a growing boy's stomach to be empty," Logan counters. This causes all of us to chuckle and makes his mood even brighter. His energy is a happy sunshine yellow, and it's infectious.

"Let's get going, and maybe we can find some of that cake pizza on the way back," I say, while I go and gather Hurri's tack. I don't need to take anything for Red and Ash, but Hurri and Storm need to be saddled.

Cass and Grey make quick work of helping, and before long we are marching out of the barn and into the meadow.

There's a tree line in the distance, and I can just make out the flaming auburn color of a horse's coat. The shadows circle him, and I know Ash is near.

When we approach the trees, Red and Ash stand side by side in Arion form. Together they look like fire and smoke, two deadly forces of nature, ready to be wielded at a moment's notice. All that training spent with Gunner this morning has nothing on the two warhorses in front of me. They exude power and grace. I can feel the presence of strength. I know they can take out thousands of soldiers. If there was a doubt in my mind before about winning this, there isn't now.

"What is Red doing out here with a gray horse?" Grey asks, looking between the two Arions.

"Do you forget that I can communicate with you? Please feel free to direct any questions my way, as to make it quicker for clarification," Red responds back to Grey. His horse face gives away nothing, but I can feel his annoyance.

"Yeah. Sorry, horse. I forgot about the whole Mr. Ed thing," Grey says in a snarky tone. I see Red's nostrils flare, and a beat of energy picks up. I have no idea if he knows the reference Grey is trying to make, but I cut it off before it can go further.

"That's enough, guys. We're here for a reason. Red, Ash, please show Grey, Cass, and Logan why you requested we come down," I say, stepping out of the way a bit. I reach out for Shax's hand, as we turn to watch them explain.

"Very well, but since this one is no longer human and cannot die easily anymore, I will not be holding back if he decides to make another rude comment toward me or my mate. I do not care if he is your knight. He should respect your soul-bonded," Red says as he steps closer to Ash, and the magical shimmer begins to overtake them. When the bright light clears, in their place are two fully clothed Fae. Red's auburn coat is now only shown on the top of his head and along his jawline in the form of a beard. His eyes are still the same penetrating ones he has as an Arion, but his body is built for battle. He's massive. There are muscles on top of other muscles. He's dressed in what seems to be battle leathers, just like the guards were wearing outside of the training yard today. Ash's gray hair is piled high atop her head with a long braid swinging down her back. She's in matching female leathers, and it leaves little to the imagination when it comes to her figure. Her face is petite and delicate, but the rest of her is toned, and fierce. She's a protector, a true guardian. Her beautiful black eyes settle on me, and she wastes no time in enveloping me in a hug. I embrace her back, even though I feel the worry coming off of Cass and Grey.

"What the fuck, Azra? Red? Gray horse-lady?" Grey questions. I have to give it to these two, they really know how to make him speechless.

"Red can shift when he's in Faerie. Even though his true form is a horse, his shifted form is a man. Ash is Shax's soul-bonded, Arion, and she's Red's mate," I explain to the guys. I can feel the jealousy roll off of Cass. He's disappointed that Storm isn't an Arion. I walk up to him and slide my hand in his. I look up into his face and smile. He leans down to kiss me, and that pang of sadness dissolves when our lips make contact.

Everyone is super special. Wow, Azra. Maybe you should just paint these giant targets on our backs saying, "SUPER REJECTS COME TO FUCK SHIT UP". Then, we wouldn't have to hide anything from anyone. Lucy and Mikey would be able to know who it is that wants to take them out, Grey projects. He's starting to pace around the trees, almost as if he is looking for an answer somewhere.

Would you stop being an ass for two minutes and come back over here and speak to us? Yes, ok. I agree that whoever follows me turns into something a little extra, but I promise you, I'm not doing it on purpose. I didn't choose this life. I didn't choose to be the Changer and have to make all these important decisions in a world I know nothing about. I'm stuck here, just like you, Grey. We need to figure shit out so that we can free humanity from the arrogance and pain of these two rulers. We need to make a better life for us...and for Logan, I say the last part looking down at the boy. He's standing directly in front of Red, staring up at him with the hugest worship eyes. His fingers are poking at the leathers, and Red's doing a very good job of ignoring him. A smile cracks across my face.

"Logan, stop poking Red. He's still Red, just in a man size," I tell him, trying to stifle a giggle. Red looks so hard-core, and Logan is just too adorable for words.

"Az, he's like a superhero. Do you think he could be in the X-Men? Wolvie and Red saving the day," Logan says, jumping around and showing awesome superhero poses. This gets a huge smile out of Red, and my giggle turns into a full-blown laugh. The rest of the group can't keep it in either, and we all join in on the fun.

Wiping away tears from my eyes, I say, "Shax and Ash need to complete their bond. Let's walk over to the waterfall and get started. I don't like being out here where just anyone can stumble upon us."

$\mathcal{I}$ hear the rush before I see it, as it comes into view with the moonlight reflected off of the falls. The pool is clear and inviting. I can feel the temperature dip as we near the edge. If I was alone with my mates, I would have suggested a group skinny dipping party. Imagining all that hot flesh pressed against mine in the cool water is doing all types of delicious things to my insides.

Ash goes to the water, shifts into her Arion form and then walks into the pool. Shax comes up behind me and gives me a quick kiss on the cheek then goes to her. They enter the water together as Red hands Shax the ingredients for the ceremony. Red comes and stands with me as we watch the ceremony unfold. Being on the outside this time makes it all the more beautiful. I can see the energy dancing around them, forming the barrier. When they exchange the blood, the color shoots into a bright purple. Plunging into the water is quick for them, and Shax wastes no time coming to the surface.

I greet him at the water's edge and wrap him in a hug. "How do you feel?" I ask, as he shakes off some of the water. He looks absolutely edible in a wet shirt clinging to all his muscles. Cass steps up to us and uses air magic to dry Shax and I off.

"I'm ok. The connection that I had with her before feels so intense now. I feel like she's an extension of me, while before it just felt like she was with me," he explains.

"I get that. I think it's meant for us to be better in battle, or that's what Red has told me. I guess time will tell," I say, with a bit of sadness in my voice. I wish I could have met them all at a different time. I wish we didn't have to deal with a war.

"I think it is best if we head back to the palace. Ash and I need to make sure we are hidden from the Queen, so we will be returning in horse form. Would you like to ride back?" Red asks.

"Sure. It will be quicker, and we brought horses for everyone," I respond.

"Tomorrow, we must work on your flying and portal magic. I understand that they have Gunner teaching you swords and combat. I would like to make sure you are able to appropriately use the magic that no one else has. You need to train your wings to carry you over distances and learn how to create the portals in Faerie," Red says.

"Really? You can teach me how to fly?" I ask in amazement.

"Yes, I know the principles, and I think your instincts will kick in once we get started," he replies. Both he and Ash shift back into their horse forms at that moment, and we make our way back to the palace.

I'm glad that Shax was able to complete his bond. Being more in sync with Ash will be beneficial when we have to make the hard choices in battle. I just hope there aren't too many.

14

PREPARING FOR THE INEVITABLE

*S*unshine streams through the curtains on the balcony. As I slowly awaken, I can hear the birds chirping and smell coffee coming from the other room. My eyes are still closed, but I can feel Shax next to me. His breathing is still heavy, and his soft snores are an indication that he's still fast asleep.

They had a new bed waiting for us last night. It's so large that it can easily fit five adults—with wings. The comfortable down filling cover cradles my body. I could spend all day here. I roll over onto my side and crack an eye open. Shax is sleeping on his back with the quilt pulled up to his stomach. His bare chest is on full display, and it looks so inviting. I lift a hand to gently caress the small amount of hair there. He's sculpted like a model, with dips and curves forming muscles. His skin is tanned, and there are intricate tattoos on both of his arms. He looks sexy sleeping like this. Before I can talk myself out of it, I shimmy down beneath the covers and straddle Shax's legs. I keep the sheet over my head, as I pull down the waistband of his boxers. I flick my tongue out and run it up his already hard cock. I love that he's ready to go, even in his sleep. I get to the tip and place it in my mouth, gently sucking as I go down. He lets out a moan, and I look up to see if he's awake. He cracks one eye and gives me a sly smile before closing them again and leaning his head back in ecstasy. His hands come up to cradle my head, threading his fingers through my hair. He gives a little tug as I suck harder and faster.

Before long, I taste the saltiness of his pre-cum in my mouth. His fingers start to massage my head, and his hips buck up to meet me. I increase my speed, moving my head up and down the length of him. Grabbing his balls with one hand, I brace myself on the bed with the other. I caress them and hum around his cock at the same time. His body tenses, and his release is fast and loud. He comes down the back of my throat, and I rise up to meet his face. His eyes are open now, and he looks happy and satisfied.

"Good morning. How did you sleep?" I ask him as I lay across his chest. I can hear his heartbeat in my ear. It's a bit quicker than normal.

"It's a good morning. I got woken up in the best way possible. You're amazing, you know that?" He responds, stroking his hand down the side of my face. Laying here with him is making me have all these girly feelings. The excitement of something like love is fluttering in my chest.

"Well, I don't know about that, but I do know that I need some coffee and food before we need to go see the ninja warrior this morning," I say, jumping up from the bed and grabbing the robe I left on the chair last night. I pad over to the bathroom and take care of business before I join Shax and the guys in the lounge.

Everyone is seated at the table eating and drinking. The mood is light this morning, and I see a bit of hope and possibility for the first time. We've all been through so much in the past week that it feels good to just enjoy each other before the day starts. It makes me think of all the mornings we can have like this in the future; if we ever get through this mess.

"Morning, Azra. How did you sleep?" Cass asks, while rising from his chair, and holding out one for me. He places a gentle kiss on my head as I lean into him. He's freshly showered and smells like frost and light. I pour myself a cup of coffee, add the appropriate amount of creamer, and lay back to enjoy it.

"Well, thanks. That new bed is amazing. I can't wait for us all to fill it," I say with a sly smile as I put the cup up to my mouth and take a sip of the magical beans. Shax gives a wide smile. He's going to be the first to partake in a little swordplay.

"Az, that's kinda gross. I know you guys are like all in love, but I don't want to hear these things," Logan exclaims. I almost spit out my coffee at his observance. He's a smart little bugger.

"Sorry, Wolvie. I'll try to keep the adult speak for when you aren't in the room," I say.

"Ok, what's the plan for today? I was thinking since we need to go see that prick of a Fae, I might get in on this battle training. It seems I'm going to have to go bat for you in this war, and I need to be able to kill Fae and help protect you," Grey confesses. He has a look of determination in his eyes. I feel the thin line between revenge and acceptance for what he is. He still needs to embrace his Fae side.

"I think that's a good idea since up until a few weeks ago we were both human, or at least I thought I was," I say, with a bit of excitement. I think having Grey to back me up will help with my training. I don't trust Gunner and his tricky magic. He may have a motive all his own. He's either going to be an ally or an enemy. The only problem is...will he be my mate?

The training building is the same as it was yesterday. Guards outside in their armor and the challenge in the air. Gunner is setting some obstacle courses up when we enter. He doesn't notice us at first, but my magic and I do. His shirt is off, and his muscles flex as he picks up a heavy hay bale and stacks it on top of another. His pants are low slung on his hips, and you can see the slight "v" just under his abs. My mind clouds over for a moment, and I can't think of anything else as my magic takes over. I snap out of it just in time, before his magic can latch on to mine. When my eyes focus again, I see him staring intently at me. His green eyes are ablaze like emeralds, so impossibly green they could never be considered ordinary. I can feel the tension in the air, and it's so much worse than it was yesterday.

"Azra, are you ok?" Shax asks, with a worried tone. His gentle touch on my shoulder brings me back to the present.

"Yes, um...I'm fine. The magic is just getting a little hard to control. I don't know how much longer I can keep it from mixing," I respond truthfully. Someone better come up with a way to shut it down. I might not be able to hold it in much longer.

"I'm going to drop off Logan with Anna. I'll be back before training is over. I saw a library on our way back the other day, maybe they'll have something in there to fix this... problem we are having," Cass says. If anyone can find an answer, it's him. I give him a quick kiss and Logan a hug before walking off to meet Gunner.

"Morning," he says with a look so sensual that it could melt panties. His chocolate hair is messy atop his head, the curls arching in usual circles waiting to be touched. His tattoos are on full display, his chest and arms bulging with intricate designs. There is a wolf over his heart that looks so real I have to do a double take to make sure it isn't moving.

"Morning," I reply. His appraisal of me is just as deep as mine is of him. His energy is gently stroking the outer parts of mine, and I quickly lash out to snap his back into place.

"Where did you learn that?" He asks, with his head slightly tilted to one side. His eyes hold mischief, and his smile holds promise.

"Learn what?" I retort. "How to get you to stop fucking with my magic? I don't know, I'm just sick of you pushing at my boundaries when I clearly don't want you to. I have three mates; I don't need a fourth."

"Yes, you do. And not only am I 'pushing your boundaries' I'm trying to see if you can shield. Your mate over there has that power, and since you turned him Fae, I figured you did too, I was just testing my theory," he replies.

"You mean the thing Grey did when we fought the dragon?" I ask.

"I killed the dragon, you tried to fly. Big difference," Grey corrects, in his sarcastic tone. This makes me turn around and stick my tongue out at him. Fucking cheeky bastard.

"Whatever, you all know what I mean. The invisible shield that Grey projected when the dragon was spitting his fire. That shield. You think I can do that because I smacked your magic?" I question.

"You not only blocked it, but you sent it back. The first half of training today is going to be physical. We will continue on with combat and sword training, and then the second part we can focus on your magic."

"Don't you think we should all teach her our own magic? I mean, you definitely can't conjure my fire, and I can't your earth. Cassiel's lightning is unique too. I think this should be a joint effort. As much as I hate that, it's what's best for Azra," Shax says with a princely tone. He's not going to budge on this. I feel some of his alpha dominance come through the bond, and Grey grits his teeth. If Shax wasn't so powerful, Grey would be my next guess for alpha.

"You have a point, Prince. If the Queen wants the Changer at her best, we need to give her everything she needs," he says with a bit of heat in his tone. He's walking a fine line between flirting and testing Shax's patience.

"Keep it in your pants, assassin. The only ones that are giving Azra everything are her mates," Shax rebukes.

"Exactly," Gunner says, as he strolls away to the weapons. I can feel the tension rolling off the guys. This is going to be some fun training.

We spend the rest of the morning fighting with various weapons. My Changer sword is my favorite though. It fits so nicely in my hand, and when I use it, it's like an extension of myself. I'm not very good yet, but I think eventually I will be able to take care of myself. Grey got in on the action too. He took up learning the bow and arrow very quickly. Shax showed him how to stand correctly and how to line up the target. By the third shot, he was already hitting the inner ring. He's a natural.

"Ready for earth magic training?" Gunner asks after we have had lunch. The two guards from outside the doors had wheeled in a large cart with various types of food and drink. After expending all that energy, I was starving. Now, in a bit of a food coma, I don't really want to train. I want to crawl into bed with my guys.

"Sure," I lie. "Whenever you are." I get up from our impromptu picnic at the haystacks and make my way over to Gunner who is standing near some potted plants in the far corner. It's extremely weird that there's a little bit of all the elements in here, but I guess a training facility needs to be ready for everything.

"First thing you are going to do is try to find your magic. You have to get to the part of yourself where it comes from and pull a little out at a time. Project it in your mind, where you want it to go, and then release. Don't use too much, or you'll probably blow something up," he says. I roll my eyes and make a get-on-with-it face. "Then push that energy into the plant, and make it bloom."

"Thanks for all that confidence," I say with a smirk on my face. Some teacher he is. Looking for the place where the bonds are, because they are the strongest magics, I have, I find the pool of energy in my center. It's a blend of all different colors, one more beautiful than the other. I begin to mentally draw from the pool, using a tiny piece and spinning it into a rope. It reminds me of taffy, thick and solid, but can be pulled into thin pieces.

The rope forms into a beautiful red color. I push it down my arm a little, and out of my fingers. I can see the energy leave my finger and jump onto the plant. It engulfs it and begins to seep down into it. The red mixes with the green color of the stem, highlighting its outline, so it almost looks like it is encased in shiny rubies. The plant's own energy begins to hum, and a loud pop sounds as the plant explodes. I jump back a little not wanting to get zapped by my own magic.

"I killed it," I say, looking down at the dust where there was once a plant.

"You certainly did. Seems like you don't have any of my magic yet," Gunner explains. His professor-like tone is in full effect, and I'm a little insulted by his lack of empathy. I tried my hardest.

"And she never will!" Grey yells from the other side of

the room. Shax is standing next to him looking just as formidable.

"Let's continue, shall we?" Gunner asks. I don't think his eyes could roll more into the back of his head.

We try to work on my earth magic for the better part of an hour. I've got nothing. The only thing the comes out from my magic pool is the lightning and fire. I try to explain that I only received my other powers when I mated with the others, but he doesn't believe me. He thinks that just being near each other should be enough.

Cass returns to us just as I'm finishing up with Gunner. He walks into the room looking extremely disappointed. His eyes are set, and his jaw is ticking. Cass isn't usually mad, so this is something of a shock.

"What's wrong?" I ask with a concerned tone. I hope that anything hasn't happened, or worse, something is about to happen.

"That whole damn library full of books, and I couldn't find one thing to stop a mating. There isn't a lot on Changer lore, but everything I read confirms what he said. In order to make the shift in power, you need a fourth mate. All four elements need to be in alignment in order for it to work. We need him, Azra," Cass says, defeated. He doesn't want Gunner any more than the rest of the guys.

"It's ok, we can look elsewhere. Don't beat yourself up because the first attempt failed," I say, while walking toward him and opening up my arms for a hug. He feels so good next to me. I want to bury myself in him and drift off to sleep.

"You won't find anything. I don't know how many times I have to say this, I'm your mate, Azra. There is no running from this. You need to accept the fact that we need to win this war together, the five of us. You trying to do it half-assed is stupid and will get you killed," Gunner spits out. It seems that his patience is wearing thin, and I couldn't give two fucks about it.

"Listen, I don't care what the magic or universe wants. If my mates say you're evil and not to trust you, then that's what I'll do. You're a killer. Someone who does the Queen's bidding at a moment notice. You killed Sola! How is that something I am supposed to accept?" I yell. I'm trying my hardest to hold on for the guys. I know Gunner is this bad guy, but my magic is screaming at me. It's starting to get painful.

"You have no clue what you are talking about. The difference between me and them is light years apart. Shax has no idea what happened that night, and Red is a fucking stuck-up prick. Don't think for one second that the decisions I make every day are easy. Do you think I enjoy this? That I enjoy killing for someone else? Confession, I don't, but I'm very good at it, and that puts a target on my back just as big as yours," he shouts. I can feel the anger pulsing off of him. His words hit my soul, and I begin to doubt myself.

"That was a pretty fucking speech, dude. You really got me with the confession part, but it still doesn't prove who you are. Azra is one of the most important things to me. I will not let her be vulnerable with a Fae fucker who kills other people's sisters, regardless if you wanted to or not," Grey counters. His posture is relaxed, but the rage and anger he carries with him wants out. It is evident in how his wings are fluttering, and his fists are clenched at his sides. His eyes stay pinned on Gunner, and for a brief moment, I feel like he might actually hit him.

"Fuck you, bird boy. Azra, when you come to your senses, ask Shax where to find me. I'm not going to keep doing this every day. My magic wants you. It wants to make you mine, but if you don't want that, then I can't be around you. It's too hard to control. We'll be fucking screwed when Michael gets here, but what does Faerie mean to you? Not like you actually give a shit," Gunner spits out while walking away from us. My mouth is hanging open at his statement. Of course, I care. How could he say that? But he doesn't know me. He knows nothing of what we are trying to do. I must look like a stuck-up spoiled brat to him.

15

COLLISION

$\mathcal{T}$he next morning Gunner is a no show. The building feels empty without his presence. Even though I'm supposed to hate him, my magic is calling to him. Instead of wasting the day, Shax and Cass take it upon themselves to show me how to use their powers. Fire magic is easier for me to conjure than the lightning or the wind. Shax assumes because he's alpha that I'm able to channel it better. I think it's because I have an affinity for it. It feels more natural in my hands, the heat of the flames and the cracking of desire to burn. Lightning feels cool and the surge of electricity vibrates through my body, like I'm charged up.

Three hours into it, my magic is spent, and the guys are exhausted. I haven't figured out how to control the amount of output yet, so basically, all the haystacks are burnt to a crisp, and all the targets that are used for combat have lightning burns. It was a productive day, but I'm exhausted.

"Do you want to take a break? I think I might need some food in order to replenish my energy," I ask. They are both laying down on the floor staring up at the ceiling. Shax taught me how to conjure his fireballs and throw them. They aren't very big, but it could be an excellent distraction or knock someone on the ass. Cass has shared how to get a spark out of my fingertips, good for close combat where I can electrocute someone.

"Lunch should be here shortly. Greyson should also be back from his meeting in a bit. Anna is willing to keep Logan with her for the duration of this battle. She's truly a good Fae. I think that it's best for Logan, even if Greyson is having issues with letting him go," Cass says with a bit of concern in his voice. Logan has wiggled his way into all our hearts. He's our little brother now, someone we should be protecting. Grey is finally realizing the danger Logan could be in should he be anywhere near the battle.

"Anna is a kind Fae. She works with a lot of children who have lost parents, or whose parents are just neglectful. She will take good care of Logan," Shax says, reassuring us all.

The guards walk into the room at that moment pushing a cart of food. The smells are delicious, and my mouth starts to water from it. I'm the first one up and at the table. I smile kindly at the guards, but all I get is a mean stare and a partial eye roll in return. Apparently, not everyone thinks I'm special.

"I can't believe I left him there! With a Fae! I must be out of my mind. What if he gets hurt? What if they bully him?" Grey shouts as he walks through the door. His face is red, and he's having a hard time controlling his anger. I place the sandwich I was about to eat down and go to him. His energy is all over the place, so I try to help him calm down.

"It's what's best for him. You know how dangerous this all is. What if someone takes him, or he gets caught in the middle? What if he gets hurt because of us? You would never forgive yourself, and neither would the rest of us. He's with Anna and the rest of the boys. He's safe and being looked after. This isn't the Light, Grey. We need to move on from that," I say while grabbing his bicep and looking into his eyes.

He stares back at me, and before I can think too much on it, he has me in a possessive kiss. Throwing all his emotions into it. His big hands tangle in my hair as he pulls me incredibly close. His reaction to our joining is instant, and I can feel his hard cock pressed against my stomach. I thread my fingers around the back of his neck and groan into his mouth. I can feel the other's excitement through the bond. It seems like they are all into it. I'm a bit nervous asking though.

"Azra, if you don't want us to all fuck you in this training building, you need to stop kissing Greyson like that," Shax growls, with so much heat, it goes right to my core. I turn around, and both guys are glowing in enthusiasm.

"I don't think I want to stop," I say, staring into his eyes. The look of hunger that flashes back at me pulsates the air with magic. Tendrils of all their energies shoot at me smashing into my chest. It feels like acceptance... like we are all bonded now.

That was intense, Grey says into my mind.

Yeah, it was, Shax agrees, also in my mind.

"Holy shit! Can you hear each other?" I ask, astonished.

"It seems that way," Cass surmises. "It must be another condition of the mating. When we all accepted each other, another bond was formed with us all."

I look at them, really look at my mates. They are all so powerful and dominant in their own right. How did I get so lucky to have these amazing men? The fact that we are connected and can feel each other is making all the feelings come front and center.

"I want this, more than I have wanted anything. I have been hurt in the past and being with you all together like this gives me hope that our bond will last the ages," I croak out, tears dripping down my face.

Cass walks up to me and wraps me up in one of his fantastic hugs. His ability to soothe me is uncanny. He's like a big blanket. I can feel love and joy coming from each of them. This is where I am supposed to be.

The door to the barn crashes open, and Red is standing in his human form staring at us. I am so shocked for a moment; I don't know what to do. This can't be good. "Another invasion is taking place on the oceanfront. There is a fleet of soldiers trying to get into the harbor. I had to shift to protect the children, and now everyone has seen," he rushes out. He is furious that he had to break his secret. I can feel how unsure he is. It was one of the only advantages we had.

I run to grab my sword from the table as the guys grab their weapons. Grey takes his bow, Shax his short swords, and Cass his metal-tipped staff that's made from some form of Fae material that conducts his lightning. They all look like warriors. Running down along the side of the castle toward the water, I can see the chaos that is taking place on the beach. Fae are battling others with swords and fists. There are so many of them, a feeling of dread comes over me. I've never been in battle before, and the odds are overwhelming.

"Stay behind us, Azra. We'll take care of it. Grey, you watch her since you have the least experience," Shax says, pushing his alpha powers out a bit. Grey answers with a wicked smirk and launches off the ground into the air. His brilliant white wings fan out, and he looks like a real angel —one that protects.

"Damn it, fucking stubborn mate!" Shax yells in his direction. Grey throws the middle finger over his shoulder and takes off into the fray. He immediately has his bow drawn and his arrow notched. Releasing it, he hits two Fae at once. An arrow shot so powerful; it goes through both. I see Cass to the left of me with his arm outstretched. He helped move the arrow with his air magic.

I pull the Changer sword from its scabbard and look over at Shax. "Let's go, I'm not going to promise to stay behind you the whole time, but I will be cautious. If I am being honest, I'm scared to all fuck right now," I confess to my alpha. His protection instincts go into hyperdrive, and I see his fire come to the surface.

Since I have a little bit of everyone's magic, I pull my magic from my core into my fingertips. My blade ignites with fire and lightning. "Holy shit, that's amazing! On second thought, I think I got this," I say with a little more confidence. What can go wrong when you have an electrocuted fire blade?

We run right into the thick of the action. The Fae who came off the boats seems fish-like. They all have a bluish-green skin which looks viscose in nature. There are scales and fins dotting their bodies. The outfits they wear are torn and old. They look like something out of a bad animated pirate movie. Their skills, however, are top notch. They swing their blades with precision, attacking like professional killers. This is why Michael hired them.

Shax is amazing, cutting down the fish Fae with both of his short swords. Swinging them in arches and decapitating them as he goes. Cass's staff is lit up with his electricity, and Fae are falling at his feet as he strikes them, their hearts stopping from the jolts. I look up into the sky and see Grey firing arrow after arrow at the crowd. He hits his mark every time.

A Fae dressed in ripped pants and a torn white shirt slung over one shoulder comes running at me. His war cry is loud and intimidating. I freeze for a moment in fascination. A creature like this is something I have never seen before. My magic, though, has a different instinct. The ground around us starts to shake, and the Fae loses his footing. He recovers quickly, but by then I'm ready. I raise my sword and prepare myself for the collision. It never comes. My fire and lightning jump from my sword and swings right into his chest. A yell rips from his mouth as blood and sinew can be seen through the gash.

Just as I think I'm safe, another pirate comes from my left knocking me to the ground. My sword flies out of my hand and lands on the ground a few feet away. I'm so shocked that I can't figure out what to do next. Nothing comes over me except panic. My magic tries to get out, but there's something squashing it down. The Fae on top of me is big and smells like low-tide. It makes me gag. He has a bright silver stone hanging from his throat, and it's glowing like a star. It reminds me of Michael's eyes. I try to push him off, but he won't budge. I see him lift off of me and swing down a knife. I turn at the last minute, and he slashes my arm, just below my shoulder. I scream out in pain. The wound feels like fire in my veins.

That's when I feel it—the energy I have been fighting for these last few days from Gunner. My magic reaches onto it like a life raft, and they crash together like the tide. This mating is different. The full force of the earth is packed into it, and my body explodes with light. I can see nothing except for the glow of my completed bond. All four of the guys are connected to me, and the feeling of rightness is so powerful that a roar is ripped from my lips, and my eyes squeeze shut. When the power ebbs, my eyes open, and I look around. All the Fae around me are motionless. They are all dead. The only ones standing are my guys and some of the Queen's men that were not in the direct line of the blast. It looks like a bomb when off, and I'm responsible for all of it.

Red comes rushing up to me with Ash fast on his heels. He drops down and picks me up from the blood-soaked ground. He is checking me over and shouting in my face, but I can't hear him. All I can do is feel my mate bonds and my soul-bonded. It's like they are a million miles away. I slip into the darkness and let it wash over me, feeling safe and protected in the arms of my Arion.

16

AN UNWANTED ALLY

I awake to hushed tones speaking on the other side of the room. My head is pounding, and I'm achy all over. My muscles are screaming at me with overuse. It's like I was riding for three days straight. I blink a few times to try and adjust to the light, but it's too bright. My arms feel like lead, and I can't bring them up to my face to shield my eyes. I'm so exhausted that I might as well be paralyzed.

"Can someone please close the curtain?" I croak. My voice sounds harsh and deep, like I smoked a full pack of cigarettes before speaking. I hear a scuffle, and feet fast approaching. The swish of the drapes being pulled reaches my ears, and the darkness that comes over me allows me to attempt to open them again. My eyelids slowly open, and my mates come into focus — all four of them, and none look happy.

"Is there water?" I ask, clearing my throat. It feels like the desert has taken up residence in there. Shax goes to the table and grabs the glass for me. He puts a straw in and holds it for me to sip. The cool liquid rushes down my throat, breathing new life into me. I greedily finish the whole glass before looking up at him. "Thank you."

"What you did was stupid. I told you to stay behind me and not to directly engage. You did neither of those things. When that blast rang out, and you collapsed, I thought you were gone. Azra, I can't lose you," Shax says with panic in his voice. He's thinking of his sister, but I'm not her.

"I explained this before. I will not hide behind any of you while you fight this battle. This is a war we must all win together. If we separate, we'll lose. I can feel it in my gut. Now that we are complete, I feel stronger and whole. Do you all feel different?" I ask. I hope they decided while I was asleep to like each other; would that be too much to ask?

"Different? Yes, I can feel each of you now, and our powers are greater. I can also feel Red and Ash a bit, although not as strongly as you four. You all taste different, like each of the elements, but, Azra, you taste like magic, pure, raw magic. I don't like being connected to the assassin, but he was right. We are stronger together," Cass confesses. I can see it took a lot for him to say that.

"I feel out of it. I think I used too much power causing that wave. I could sleep for a week," Grey says. He's slumped in one of the chairs by the fire. His eyes look tired, and his skin paler than normal. He's dressed in pajama bottoms, and his wings are gone. Boy, I miss the sight of them.

"What wave? Was that after I passed out?" I ask.

"Just before. A pulse of energy shot through me and, on instinct, I pushed a tidal wave over the ships. They all sunk," he replies.

"Now that we are all connected, we'll have to get used to the power boost, what you did out on the oceanfront, Azra, was nothing short of amazing, but it took a lot out of us,"

Gunner says. He's leaning in the entryway of the bedroom, neither in nor out.

"What did I do?" I ask. I'm confused as to how they are all exhausted when I'm the one who set an Azra bomb off.

"You siphoned our magic to make an energy bomb. Now that we're all connected, you have the ability to use all of our magics at will. I didn't know it would come so easily to you. I thought we'd have to practice it, but all it took was the final mating. This is a far greater power than anyone anticipated," Gunner replies. He looks over at Shax who seems to be vibrating with anger. The rest of them are as well.

"Anticipated? Who anticipated? You, or my mother? Which one of you is the concoctor of this fucking scenario? Explain to us what my mother has sent you to do. Tell us now, once and for all, *mate,* what she wants done. This way, when you slit one of our throats like you did my sister's, we'll know why," Shax spits out. The anger is rolling off of him in waves, and it is beginning to heat the room. The temperature starts to shift, and if I don't stop it, the room will light up.

"Shax, calm down. I already set one room on fire. I don't need you to do the same," I say while grasping at his hand. He looks down at me, and the pain and hurt in his eyes is evident. He doesn't want to be here in this situation, but he would do anything for me. "Why don't you start from the beginning and explain to us why you're really here. I don't buy for a second that the Queen sent for you. Since we're all mates and will all need to get along to defeat Michael, let's get this all out in the open."

I move up on my hands to pull myself up to a sitting position as Cass comes behind me and adjusts the pillows to make me comfortable. I smile up at him, and he places a soft kiss on my forehead. Gunner comes into the room then, accepting his role, and takes a seat opposite Grey.

"I'm here for you, Azra. I got the mating call as soon as you stepped into Faerie. I'm an Earth Fae. My powers aren't only about earthquakes and plants. I have a vast connection with Faerie. I can see every life force on it, and when you came through the portal, yours shot right to me, calling me to it. We're made for each other, Azra, even if you hate me," Gunner says with a bit of longing in his eyes. He is speaking the truth now, but why lie before?

"Is that how you're a good assassin? You can see life forces like pegs on a map? All the people and beings around you. Can you pick out individual ones, or is it just all random?" I ask, curious to know the extent of his power. I'd love to be able to use this against Michael somehow. If we could know where he is at all times, it would mean everything to winning this war.

"Yes, and no," he replies while running a hand through his dark hair. His arm flexes at the movement, and the tattoos on his forearm dance. I can't wait to see them all. "I can look for people if I have a connection to them, or if I have something they desire. What makes me a good assassin is that I'm good at killing things. My powers just help that."

Again, the truth. He's trying to lay it all out for me. "Why lie to me at our first meeting? You felt my energy jump toward yours. Why make up a story about the Queen?"

"Red and Ash were with you, and I froze. If he knew you were my potential mate, he would have killed me right there, and I needed to make you see me first before everyone started showing you who they think I am."

"Are you trying to tell us that you're not the assassin that killed the cat's sister?" Grey asks in a condescending tone.

"Alright, Grey. Stop being an ass. He's trying to explain to us what this all means. So far, he's the only one out of the five of us that has a fucking clue as to what is going on," I say, holding up my hand. It drops down of its own accord a second later, but at least it paused his rant. "Continue, Gunner."

"It's not easy being the Dark Assassin. I'm not expecting pity, or even understanding, but I've been ostracized and, on the outside, looking in for centuries. No one will even be friends with me, let alone mate with me, so when I found you, and you were real, and strong, and beautiful, I lied," he says, wiping his hand across his face in a shy gesture. I'm getting nothing but nervous energy from him right now.

"I'm not like those Fae. I'm different. If you would have explained, I would have heard you out," I say, gently.

"That's the first lie I have heard you tell, Azra," Gunn says, shaking his head in disbelief. "You didn't know who I was until later, and the first thing you did was reject me because someone else told you not to like me. You acted like the rest, and that's why I didn't confide in you about anything. That's why I am having a hard time trusting you now."

"I...um...I don't know what to say. You're right. I did judge you, and it's mainly because I trust my mates and my soul-bonded with my life. I followed them blindly when I should have made my own choice. For that, I am sorry," I say with pleading eyes. If I could go to him I would, but instead, I send out a desire for him to be near me through the bond. He moves from the doorframe and takes a seat on the bed with me. I place my hand on his, and I just stare into his face for a moment. He has hurt there, in his heart. He's looking for his place in this world, and the only person who can understand that is me. As his mate, I need to be able to make him feel at home. I open my arms as wide and as far as I can before they tire, and he slips into the space between them. This hug is awkward and uncomfortable, but it's a start. A sigh of relief washes over him, and I extend that feeling to all the guys. They need to know his pain and recognize we should never feel alone if any of us is around.

He gets up from the bed and gives me a small smile. Just before he leaves the room, he turns back to me and says, "You called me Gunn."

"Yeah, everyone gets a nickname," I say, with a smirk. He nods his head and leaves.

*t takes me four days to recover from the Azra bomb. Four long lazy days of being in bed, eating, and reading. If I push everything to the side for a moment, I feel like I'm on the best beach vacation ever. Then reality smacks me in the face, and it becomes apparent we're fighting a war.

"What's all that shouting?" I ask, putting my book down and hopping off the bed. I go to the window and see the commotion in the courtyard below. There are guards everywhere, and there seems to be a small brigade dressed in the color of the Light. Fuck, this can't be good.

I go back in my bedroom and get dressed. Clothes in Faerie are weird, but I find something like leggings and a long tunic. I put up my long inky hair into a messy bun and throw on some riding boots. The guys are all sitting in the lounge watching some sort of Faerie TV. It's like regular TV, but it's all in 3D holograms. It creeped me out the first time they showed it to me, so I choose to read instead.

"Did you all not hear the noise outside?" I ask, waiting by the front door. They all turn to look at me like they are being ripped from a dream. I see what they are watching and quickly understand why. It's some crazy action movie, with dragons, war, and other boy things.

"Where are you going?" Shax asks.

"It seems we have visitors because there's a bunch of army men in the courtyard wearing Michael's colors. I'm going to check it out. I don't want to be the last to know if it's something important," I say.

Shax rises from his chair and makes his way over to me, pulling his shoes on as he goes. Grey, Gunn, and Cass do the same. We make our way down to the courtyard where everyone is still congregating. The Queen hasn't shown up yet, but the crowd all parts for Shax, and we come face to face with all the commotion.

"What the fuck are you doing here?" I ask in astonishment. On top of a beautiful gray mare is Daniel, Cass's brother. He's dressed in full armor like he is prepared for battle. There are at least twenty men with him, and they all look like they are ready to attack at a moment's notice. My magic instantly goes on alert, and I pull some toward my chest. I hear a hiss behind me that reminds me to not pull too much energy, or I will hurt the guys.

"Azra, easy," Gunn says in my ear. He grabs my arm in a light gesture, and it calms me down a bit. I shrug out of his grip, not wanting Daniel to know all our secrets.

"Daniel, what are you doing here?" Cass says as he steps in front of me in a protective gesture. His energy is pulsing, and I can feel the uneasy feelings rolling off of him. Daniel gives his brother the biggest smirk, adding fuel to the fire.

"Brother, how good to see you! I've come to help and offer my services to give the Changer a chance to beat our father," he says with a smile. His eyes roam over me, running up and down my length. I hear a growl, and anger flares through the bond. Grey walks up and stands beside Cass, blocking my view from Daniel.

"Ah, the human. We wondered where you went!" Daniel exclaims with glee, like he found his special toy again. His sinister grin makes me want to punch him.

The air charges with magic, and before I can say anything, Grey has the water from the fountain around the prince's head, suffocating him in a bubble. Everyone around us watches in astonishment as Daniel tries to pull the water away from his face.

"That's enough, Grey," I yell, pulling on his arm. It doesn't faze him, as his gaze is locked on the prince. He's hyper-focused. I try again, and he's still ignoring me. I reach inside me and pull the magic I know is Grey's toward me. He stumbles back into me, and the bubble bursts around Daniel's head. He starts coughing and spitting water out of his mouth and nose. His face turns a brilliant shade of red, and he eyes train on Grey.

"You are fucking dead," he spits out. He tries to dismount his horse, but the guards point their amber guns at him. Grey keeps a steady eye on him, and I can feel his anger pulsing. He wants Daniel dead, and I can only imagine the reasons why.

"I wouldn't get down off that horse if I were you. I also wouldn't threaten one of the Changer's mates," Shax says nonchalantly. He's cool on the outside, but raging below the surface is a ball of energy waiting to strike Daniel if he moves the wrong way.

"Mates? Azra, what is this Dark mongrel talking about? You mated with a human? With this hunter? No matter. I'm here for you; here only for you. I want to speak with you privately. Can you please tell these goons to back off?"

Daniel says, while wiping water out of his hair. He looks pissed. I wonder why he's really here.

"Our dear Azra may be the Changer, but I am the Queen," a voice calls out as she walks down the palace steps into the courtyard. A collective breath is held as she descends. All Fae in the court bow down to her, and Shax tugs on my sleeves as he kneels.

Azra, it's not the time. Please, he says through the bond. I look into his eyes and realize he's right. There will be a time and place for it. I kneel beside my mates but don't bow my head. I will never turn my back on the Queen. She sees me standing out from the rest as she walks past. A savage smile is placed upon her lips, and it echoes the challenge that is there.

Daniel dismounts his horse and kneels before the Queen. The rest of the small army he brought with him does the same. "Why are you here, Prince? Michael should know I do not negotiate. He should know that he signed your death warrant the moment you rode through my gates," she says.

"Your Majesty. It is a great honor to meet you. I am not here at the behest of the King. I am here for the Changer. I want to help. My father has gone mad and has killed my mother. He can no longer be trusted. I want to see him burn for his sins. The Dark should get their chance to rule Earth, and I know how it can be done," he confesses. His head is still bowed, so I can't see his face, but his posture says it all —he's grieving. I feel Cass through the bond, and his heartbreak is apparent. He hasn't dared move from his position, but I can feel him starting to lose control. I reach through the bond and try to console him while I can't get to him, but it's not enough.

"You're here for your revenge? To avenge your mother?"

she asks. Her smile is broadening. She loves his suffering and to watch him squirm.

"Yes, Your Majesty. I am here to seek revenge and to help the Dark win," he replies. No one has moved from the moment she came out of the palace. There are no sounds except the wind and a few birds chirping in the trees. The sun is high in the sky, and the balmy temperature is making me sweat. It feels like forever before she opens her mouth to speak.

"You won't mind then if I kill all your men?" she asks, having to prolong his suffering by taking something else. He shifts from one knee to the other, clearly uncomfortable with making this decision. Before he has too, Shax speaks up.

"Perhaps we can keep them as collateral or even have them work for us? I don't see the sense in killing good soldiers when we have a war to fight, Mother," Shax says. His mask is back on, and he looks forever the prince.

"Too true, son," she thinks out loud. "There might be use for the extra bodies. We may need them to die for us. Bring the soldiers into the barracks and get them sorted with new uniforms and into the right battalions. If there is a question of your loyalty, speak it now, and you will get a quick death. Because if I find out that you have betrayed me later on, you will pray for your suffering to end."

"Your Majesty. May I be permitted to stand?" Daniel asks.

"Rise! All of you!" She shouts. She's done here. As he stands before her for the first time, he looks scared shitless. She's not a tall woman, or even a scary looking one, but her power is crushing. It makes you feel like you are so powerless.

"You say you are here to defy your father. Fine. Give me

something that could crush him, and then I may let you live," she demands.

"His army is about a week's ride from here in the Snowcap Mountains. He plans to lead them down here in one month's time. The dragon assassin was only for a distraction. He wanted you out of the Dark Court because the Summer Palace is easier to overthrow, or so he says."

The Queen's jaw ticks with rage. The violet in her eyes flares, and I know someone is about to die. A tree in the courtyard is engulfed in flames, and a guard standing next to it is swallowed along with it. The fire is so intense, they are instantly turned to ash. Another life lost because she can't keep her temper in check. This needs to stop.

"You may stay...for now. But know this, Prince, if you dare to defy me, I will cook you from the inside, starting slowly with your organs, and leaving your brain for last, so that you can feel and see all that is happening to you before you die."

Daniel's face goes pale as he bows his head once again. A cold chill washes over my body, and I feel the wrongness in the air. She's a sick woman. I move over to Cass and take his hand. He just found out his mother died, and he can't even grieve how I know he wants to. Turning around to us, she gets right in my face.

"Find out what the boy's real motivation is, and then get rid of him," she threatens in a whisper too low for anyone else to hear. Our eyes are locked in a staring game, and the nudge through the bond from Shax makes me lower them first. I can't wait to destroy this bitch.

Satisfied with my submission, she walks away in a flourish of skirts and evil. I turn to Cass and wrap my arms around him. He nuzzles my neck and seeks comfort hidden there. He's going to be a mess when we get to our rooms.

"You got this, just until we are inside. Then you can let go," I whisper in his ear. He nods his head in agreeance and removes himself from our embrace.

"Sorry to have you hear how mother died like that. I wanted to tell you in private," Daniel says, with a flash of true pain in his eyes. I don't doubt that he did love his mother.

"Let's take this inside. There's a meeting room we can use to hash out the details of this agreement. Cass and Azra can go up to our rooms while we negotiate a deal," Shax suggests, looking at the rest of my mates and Daniel. All men silently agree as we begin walking toward the palace. I glance over at Daniel and can't shake the feeling like something is seriously wrong out of my system. I don't trust he's here for revenge. I think he has motives we don't know about yet, but I intend to find out.

Cass goes straight for the room we are sharing. He removes his boots and gets on the bed. His sorrow is so powerful through our bond it's almost crippling. I take off my shoes as well and climb into bed with him.

"I'm so sorry about your mother. I didn't know her well, and I can't imagine the pain you're in right now," I whisper into his neck as I hold him from behind. He doesn't speak, but the tears begin. He breaks down for the mother he lost, and the father we'll have to kill. After over 500 years, Cass needs to face that he will be an orphan.

Hours later, the day has passed, and the moon is shining through the open balcony window. I can hear the sound of the ocean, and smell the fresh breeze coming through. Shax walks into the room with Grey and Gunn on his heels. They seem tense and anxious. This must have been some meeting.

"I assume it didn't go well?" I ask, sitting up on the bed. Cass stirs beside me and mirrors my actions.

"He's a fucking dick. No offense, Cassiel, but his pompous attitude is going to get him killed quickly. It's almost like this is a joke to him. Just another day in the life of Prince Daniel," Gunn says. He takes a seat in one of the armchairs. They all look exhausted.

"No offense taken. He's been a dick for centuries. He's an entitled brat that my mother doted over for years. It won't change anytime soon. Did he mention why he wants to see Azra?" Cass responds. He gets up from the bed and stretches his body out. He's still sorrowful, but it seems like our little cuddle helped with getting the worst of it out. Princely manners have him moving on.

"He wants to help free Noli. He said it's his ultimate sacrifice to us so that we believe him going forward. I don't see how this asshole is going to help, because he has never paid attention before, but it's up to you, Az," Grey says.

My heart does a flip flop in my chest. Noli! How could I not seize the opportunity to save her? Daniel knows exactly what he's doing. I need her back. I didn't think Michael would bring her to Faerie. I thought she was still trapped in the Light on Earth.

"That fucking fucker," I say. "This is really the only way we'll definitely work with him. He's exploiting my feelings for her."

"That's what we said to him. But, Azra, it's your decision to make. You know I'll follow you anywhere, but is it worth it to possibly get caught because of your friend?" Shax asks. I see red at that moment. The air in the room starts to whirl in a tornado-like fashion. My hair lifts from my shoulders.

My eyes glow an intense grey. The storm has come. How dare he imply Noli isn't important. He has no idea!

"I will never leave my friends behind. She has been my life for these last two years. She's the reason I survived. I would never let Michael keep her if I had the chance to save her. Just as I would never let him keep any of you!" I scream. The wind is getting violent, and I don't care. My emotions are fueling my powers, and I want to rip Michael limb from limb. I'm not the girl who left the Light court. I'm the Changer.

"Calm down! Azra, look at me! We'll find Noli. No one said we wouldn't help. You're going to harm someone, and I know you don't want to do that," Cass yells into my ear. He has his hands on my shoulders, staring into my face, and holding on to me at the same time. The other guys are braced on chairs or various pieces of furniture to help keep them from flying around the room. Cass's plea comes through the bond, and his urgency pulls me from my anger. I can't hurt my mates. I pull the magic back into me and look around the room. Everything is a mess.

"Take me to Daniel," I demand, walking out of the room. The rest follow as I walk out the door and down the hallway.

17

FREEING NOLI

*H*e's sitting in one of the parlor rooms sipping a drink and reading a book. I march right up to him and stand before him. He notices me and places his cup down. I have my hands on my hips, and the anger that is coming off of me is making the room heat. I know I must look like a wild banshee with my swirling grey eyes and lightning fingertips.

"I see a lot has happened since you left us. Mated to a human and my brother. How's that working out for you?" he teases, with a smile spread wide on his face. Back is the cocky prince.

"Shut the fuck up. You're not a prince here. You're actually a cushy prisoner. One false move, and I'll burn you alive," I snarl, lightning crackling on my fingertips. "Now, you have a single chance to tell me. Where is Noli?"

"She's at my father's camp in the mountains. She's a witch, you know. A really powerful one too. I think that's the only reason why she's still alive. That, and she seems to interest him."

A growl passes my lips as I lunge at him. I knock both him, and the chair he is perched on, to the floor. My electric hands make contact with his face, as I punch him. His mouth splits open, and blood spatters on my face. Shax is on me in an instant, pulling me off of him. I'm screaming and kicking to get back to Daniel, but Shax's grip is firm.

"You need to calm down, Azra. Don't let the magic overtake you. I know he's an asshole, but we need him," Shax whispers. "We need him to free Noli."

I take a deep breath in and try to focus my mind. He's right, my alpha, but I just can't bring myself to not want to rip Daniel's throat out. My anger is still pulsing. I look toward my mates, and I can see varying degrees of emotion from sorrow to Grey's anger.

"Tell me how to get her out. I want you to be as specific as possible. If you fail at this, I will kill you," I threaten. My hands hurt, and my head is going to explode. I need to get this aggression out somehow.

"We sneak in through the tunnels. There's an underground system that will lead us up into the mansion where he's made his home. It's not as dreary as you are thinking. Nothing my father does is half-assed. It seems that the last time he was here, he had this home built for emergencies," Daniel says, wiping the blood from his nose. He's going to have bruises all over tomorrow.

"How long will we have until they move out? And how many days will it take to get there?" I ask. My powers want out. I need to get the fuck out of here soon.

"Like I told the Queen, his plan is a month from now when you have the party. He's going to use it as a distraction to get to all of you. It takes six days on horseback to get there."

"Did you ride in on a Fae horse?" I ask as he looks at me like I'm stupid.

"Yes. There are no other types of horses here."

"We'll take Red and Ash," I say turning around and looking at my guys, ignoring Daniel's comment. "Grey can fly if it's too much. I don't care how we get there, but I need to get Noli out," I state while walking out of the room. There's nothing left to say.

"I'm coming with you!" Daniel yells at my back. I'm just at the doorway. I spin on my heels and stare at him from across the room.

"You're not going anywhere. You're going to stay and prove to the Queen that you aren't here for some nefarious reason. I'm sure she will be more than happy to play the gracious host," I say, exiting the room and not looking back. I need to go find my Arion.

Searching for him through the bond, I can feel Ash and Red are in the training building. I make my way over, shaking with tension. My energy is going nuts, feeding off my emotions. I need to calm down.

"Azra, wait up!" Gunn yells from behind me. His footsteps are soft against the grass. The sun is shining, and the briny scent of the ocean is drifting on the wind. The grounds are bustling with life, and I look around, noticing we aren't the only people here. It's hard to open up, and actually see what's going on around you when you have so much going on inside. I miss my best friend. I miss everything about her, especially her laugh and the way she used to make us pancakes and eggs when we were too hungover to go to Manny's.

"What do you want? You should be going to get ready like the rest of the guys. I know you felt my urgency just as much as they did," I say, not breaking my stride. If he's coming with me, he needs to catch up.

"Your magic is all over the place. We can't go on this journey without you trying to control it. You're five seconds away from another Azra bomb," he says. This makes me pause. I turn around and get right in his face.

"You mean to tell me for the last four fucking days we have been sitting on our asses doing nothing, when you could have explained this to me. You knew all along how to handle this, and what would happen, and you kept it from me? Your mate?" I spit out. My arms catch on fire, and the beautiful red engulfs my body. I look like a walking fireball. My eyes sparkle with my lightning, and I can hear the fountains behind us overflowing. Blazing wings sprout out of my back, and I lift up off the ground using my air magic. I look like the elements personified.

"Azra, you need to calm down. There are Fae all over. You can very well kill everyone. Is that what you want? Come down and fight me. Get the anger out. Let's get you back to normal so we can free your friend."

This gets my attention. I know he's speaking logically, but I can't calm down. Everything in me is screaming to let go. To release all of it out into the world, and deal with the consequences of it later.

"I can't. I don't know how," I say through gritted teeth. All of this power shouldn't be contained in one person. It's too much.

"Start with one piece. Let go of the air and come back down to me. I'll help with the rest."

I close my eyes and feel for Cass's magic. It's all grey and shiny like a newly minted quarter. I tug on it a bit, and it goes from a taut ribbon into a floppy one. I feel myself begin to lower. I open my eyes, and I'm face to face with Gunn. His green eyes are glowing, and I can feel his arousal through the bond. The magic is making us drawn to one another.

"That was great. Now let me help you through the rest. I'm going to touch you now. Is that ok?" he asks with his hand outstretched toward my wings. I nod in agreement and wait for him to complete his move.

The oil slick feathers that crown the tops of my wings are alight with my fire magic. Gunn pushes through the flame, and lightly brushes a hand down the left wing. He slowly drags his hand up and down sending shivers through my body. This feels more than just an act to get me to relax. This feels like...desire. He brings his other hand up to my face, and I look up at him with the lightning breaking just behind my eyes. I want to devour the world, and I want to take him with me. The urge is too great. I crush into him. Our magic collides, and a pulse is driven from us out into the world. I don't pay attention to where it goes. I don't think in this moment what this will mean or if there will be consequences. All I want is to feel Gunn on every part of me. His hands fist into my hair, and his lips devour me. My tongue invades his mouth, and we fight for dominance. A dark shadow overtakes us, and I break the kiss to look up and find out what it is. We are encased in a canopy of vines woven so tightly it's like we're in our own little world. It distracts me from the anger, and I can think a bit more clearly.

"This is beautiful," I tell him, pulling apart and looking around in amazement. He's watching me carefully, almost like this is important to him.

"Azra, we can't stay in here long," he looks to me pleading. I cock my head in one direction in curiosity. Why would he say that to me?

"Ok, so then let's hurry up," I say with a smile. It doesn't go unnoticed that I am still on fire. He reaches for me again, and our heated kiss from before starts up again. I throw myself at him, and he catches me with such grace that I feel we could be dancing in the clouds. This kiss is consuming. It's awakening something inside of me that's much bigger than Gunn and me. This is the piece that we need to beat Michael. This is my final piece.

Gunn places me down on the earth, and a beautiful bed of flowers springs up from the ground, sacrificing themselves for our union. Faerie is with us. She can feel that a change needs to be made, and she accepts us. As I touch the earth, my fire dies down, and we are encased in the darkness of this cocoon. Gunn licks and sucks on my neck slowly making his way down to my chest. He pushes my shirt up and without hesitation places a nipple into his mouth, sucking and biting it with just the right amount of pressure. His other hand finds its way to the juncture between my legs, spreading them apart to reach my sensitive nub. I am pulsing with need beneath him, and the magic that surrounds us is all-encompassing. It's creating this vortex of energy that needs to be fed by our lovemaking.

Reaching between us, I grab the hem of his shirt bringing it over his head, breaking contact for only a moment. It falls into a heap beside us, and then Gunn is on top of me again. I wish it wasn't so dark in here. I'd love to see all his beautiful tattoos again. Our pants come off next, and we are laying with one another naked. I can feel the hard press of his cock on my stomach, and my arousal increases. He begins to kiss me again with an urgent need. Lifting my hips up, I grind myself against him, letting him know I'm ready for him.

"Are you sure you're ready?" He asks, breaking from the kiss to stare at my face.

"Yes, we need to complete this bond. I need to feel whole with you inside of me," I say breathlessly. His nostrils flare as he takes in my arousal and plunges down on my lips. He sinks in between my thighs, and his cock brushes my core ever so lightly. I groan out impatiently and try to gain some friction.

"I've thought of this moment since the first time we met by the scrying pool. Once our magics touched, I knew I had to have you," he says, trailing kisses down my body. Every kiss feels like a feather caressing my skin. When he gets to my center, I spread my legs open for him, and he takes me into his mouth. His tongue flicks out and moves up and down my wet folds. Twirling in a circle when he gets to my nub. He places his lips over it and gives a gentle tug with his teeth. The sting of pain mixed with the heat of his mouth is driving me mad. He sucks and nips until I am wriggling underneath him. Placing two fingers inside me, he pumps in and out while his lips suck and make me reach that cliff. I fall down and bask in the bliss of my orgasm. My fingers clench around him, and he lets out a guttural moan to match my own. He wastes no time sliding his thick cock inside of me with a quick thrust. He works me right back up into a frenzy. I hold onto his shoulders to steady myself a bit more, wrapping my legs around his back to give him better access. He pounds into me and kisses me with abandon. The sensations that are taking over my body are consuming me from the inside. I reach my orgasm much quicker this time, squeezing his cock with my pleasure. He soon follows me and comes with a shudder of his shoulders and a moan on my breast. We lay there for a few seconds just basking in the glow of our lovemaking. I feel complete.

*R*ed and Ash are exactly where I felt them, in the training building sparing with one another. They are both so powerful and graceful. Ash wields her blade like a master with centuries of practice. They seem evenly matched, with Red grunting every time she brings her sword down on his. I wish I had a tenth of her strength. I still fight like a human.

I stand off to the side with Gunn next to me. He brushes his hand on mine, and I look up at him with a smile. It's so easy for me to get angry now, so I'm grateful to have these men in my life to ground me.

They finish up and Red turns to me, noticing there's something wrong for the first time.

"What happened?" he asks, coming over to where we are standing. Ash is right behind him with the same concerned look on her face.

"We've found Noli. She's being kept prisoner in the mountains with the King. I'm going to get her back, but I need you to take me in Arion form. Time is not on our side before he comes for us, and I need to make sure she's safe before this whole thing starts," I explain, watching his face for any sign of disagreement. There is none.

"Give me a few minutes to get everything sorted, and we'll leave right away. I'll meet you in front of the palace. Ash, will you accompany us?" he asks, turning to her and grabbing her hand in his.

"Of course, my love. I go where you go. We've been separated for too long," she answers, leaning in and giving him a quick kiss on the lips. A swell of joy blossoms in my chest. He feels my happiness through the bond, smiling at me before leaving to get everything ready.

"Let's go back and get the rest of the guys ready. We need a plan before we take on this crazy mission. I'm starting to get nervous," I say, placing my hand in Gunn's and pulling him toward the door.

The guys are already waiting for us outside when we approach the castle. There are supplies lining the ground, and Cass has my sword in its scabbard. He holds it out to me, and I strap it on my back.

"Thank you for getting everything ready," I say looking at three of my mates. Shax and Cass seem to have the mission on their minds, while Grey is standing off to the side. I walk over to him and get into his personal space. Giving him a questioning look, I ask what's wrong through the bond.

"You had sex with him," he says. "And not just any sex, sex I could feel through the bond. It's different when you are with the other two. This feels powerful. Like the two of you could light the world on fire."

"It doesn't mean my feelings for you are any less. It just means we are complete as mates. We can now make the changes that are important to help save the humans and Fae."

"I'm not insecure in your feelings for me. I get what you are feeling inside the bond. Besides, I know I'm your favorite," he says with a smirk. "But it's dangerous—the energy I feel. I believe you and I are so close in our magic because you created me. That must be why I feel it more than the others, and it scared the shit out of me. Just promise you won't freak out again and blow up the world," he says, leaning in and pulling me close. I wrap my hands around him and take comfort in his embrace. This is so unlike him, to give me his feelings so readily. I'm almost scared if I move the wrong way he will return to broody Grey.

"Are you guys ready? Red and Ash are here," Shax says, breaking us apart from our little union.

"Yes, let's start this journey. Red, are you able to carry both Grey and I? Or should he fly?" I ask, moving over to him and checking the saddle that Cass put on. Not that I don't trust him, but a rider should always check their own saddle.

"I can carry you both. Arion are superior to Fae horses. This means we can carry heavier loads, and gallop faster. Do not worry about me," he says, nuzzling into my chest. I missed my Arion. Red the man is great, but my bond is with Red the Arion. Sounds weird, but in this form, he feels like mine and not Ash's.

I hop up on Red, and Grey settles in behind me. Gunn has his own horse. He had her stabled at the Unseelie court, and he brought her with him when we left for the summer palace. She looks similar to a Fae horse, but there is something different about her. She is pure white with a shimmer to her coat. I give him a raised eyebrow saying, when-were-you-going-to-tell-me-about-her, before turning around and checking on the other guys. Shax and Cass mount Ash, and we start out. The journey for the first few hours is through the forest that lines the castle. We're going back north the way we came. The mountain range where they are holding Noli is just beyond the Dark Court's castle.

I'm enjoying riding again. The wind whipping in my face, as I feel Red's powerful gait move beneath me is invigorating. Grey's hands are tight around my waist. I don't know if he has ridden a horse this fast before. The way he is digging his hands into me makes me think he hasn't.

We ride at full speed for two days, stopping only to sleep and eat. The strength that Red and Ash have is amazing. They carry us with no problem, and Grey never has to fly. Cass and Shax ride together the whole time. I think that they are aware that Grey isn't as comfortable with them yet. Gunn's horse, Jezebel, is majestic. She keeps up with my Arion, and I wonder just what type of creature she is. Red must sense my curiosity because he laughs every time I think about it. He says she will tell me if she wants to reveal herself. I don't understand what the big deal is. Sometimes I think he does this to me on purpose.

When we get within walking distance to the mountain range, Red and Ash shift into human form. We all gear up with our weapons and wait for the cover of night to move out. Gunn hides Jezebel in the woods in a pen that he constructs of branches and leaves. It was awesome watching him work his magic. Since we consummated our mating, I have been feeling more powerful and aware of my magic. It now comes to me almost as second nature. The threads of energy surrounding us respond to me, and I can bend them to my will. I don't think anyone is prepared for what I'm capable of doing.

"Is this where Daniel said we could get in?" I ask Shax.

"Yes, there is a secret tunnel that runs under the mountain. He said that it should lead to a cavern where we can climb the stairs and be in the far corner of the dungeon. They are keeping her in the cell closest to the guards in case she gets out," he explains, looking at me for confirmation of the plan. I hate that she is there. The need to see her is an urgency I can't explain. It pushes me to hurry up and get her.

"How do we know this tunnel isn't guarded?" Grey asks.

"Daniel said that during the midnight hour there is a

shift change, and it takes them twenty minutes to fill in the gap. Once we get into the tunnel, there shouldn't be any guards. There's nothing down there except for a large room. It was used for storage, or that's what he says," Shax explains.

"I want Azra to stay with me," Red says, looking at the guys. I can see the urge to disagree on their faces, but Red's power outmatches their own, and Shax is the only one still staring into his face.

"No, she will stay with me," he grinds out. Ash walks over to him and places a hand in his to get his attention. While I should feel jealous, I only feel and see her concern. She loves him like a brother.

"Shax, listen to Red. He's a general. The one who led the army when we fought the last Changer. He's the reason why most of the Fae are still alive. If he says Azra is safest with him, then listen," Ash says, looking into his face. She's serious right now. Her don't-test-me look makes me even want to back away.

"We'll be together. There's no reason why anyone needs to be next to anyone else. It's not like some of us are staying behind," I say, chuckling just at the thought. Five sets of eyes stare back at me like I'm crazy. "Wait, you thought I wasn't going to go in there and get Noli myself? You all have another thing coming if you think I'm leaving this up to you. It's my fault that Noli is here, and I intend to get her back," I say. There's no way I'm sitting this one out.

"Az, we just want you safe," Gunn says, coming over to stand in my space. He brushes a hand over my cheek, making my face flush. I think of how his hands were all over me the last time we were alone. I take a step back and glare at him.

"I will not be seduced into staying here. I'm the most

powerful one out of all of us, and I'll stop at nothing to save her!" I shout. I'm starting to get pissed. How dare they try to make me stay out of this. My body starts to get warm, and I welcome my fire to my hands. I'm getting better about keeping it concentrated instead of setting my whole body on fire.

"This is exactly what we mean, Azra. Your emotions are leading your powers. If we go in there and something has happened to her, or happens to us, you're going to collapse that mountain. Your power is still too raw. I'm sorry, love, but this is the truth," Cass says, not moving from where he is. I know he was my first, and the one who started all these connections, but I can't help wanting to punch him in the mouth right now. Turning to Red, I look up at him.

"What do you think, General?" I say, giving him a cocky smile. I can't imagine my Arion in battle gear leading an army.

"You will stay with me, but not here. We go together, but you listen to everything I tell you. You have no experience in battle. You need to focus on staying alive for us. You can't change the world if you aren't alive. Remember that, and we should be fine," he replies, looking around at the guys, daring them to butt in. I love my Arion a bit more in this moment.

"Fine, but just know I'm not jumping behind you if there is going to be trouble. I'll get my vengeance on the King, whether it be this day or another, and I will get Noli out. Those two things are non-negotiable," I say, walking away from our group and down the hill toward the mountain.

We have the cover of night to hide our progression, but I still feel slightly exposed. I can't see any energies except for the guys and Ash, so we must be alone, but there's a nagging feeling in the back of my mind. Cass comes up to me and grabs my hand. He places a sweet kiss on my palm and smiles at me reassuringly. I don't know how he's keeping it all together. He basically lost both of his parents since I have come along.

How are you doing? I project to him.

As good as can be expected. It's funny that I should be so upset. My mother wasn't a kind Fae, nor was she a good one, but she did give me life, he replies.

That's how I felt about my mom, or who I thought was my mom. She was a terrible person, but she still kept me alive long enough to live this life.

You'll have to tell me that story one day.

I'll have to find out what really happened first. If she isn't my mother, then who is?

Good point, he says, stopping me in my tracks. We've approached the tunnel that will take us into the mountain. The air is cool and crisp with a touch of snow. The moon is bright enough that I can see where the entrance is carved into the side of the mountain. There are symbols above it, much like the ones in the door we used to escape the palace. I look over at Cass and see that he sees the same thing I do. He nods, and we both make our way over. The rest of our group follows. The symbols are indeed the same. Cass places his hand on it and uses his air magic to push some energy into the stone. Once again, it's not enough. I lean in and place my hand over his, and my pulsing red energy rushes to meet his, and the door hisses with the sound of being unlocked. It opens just enough for a hand to stick through, but Cass isn't strong enough to get in. Red takes hold of an upper portion and opens it wide enough for us to squeeze through.

The tunnel is dark and creepy. There is moisture in the air, and I feel a certain heat radiating off the rocks. Touching the walls, my palms heat up to a comfortable temperature.

"Are we in a volcano?" I ask looking at Red. He seems to be my *Fae Book for Dummies.*

"No, but it is something similar. In Faerie, there are certain mountains that contain hot water springs which heat up the whole mountain. Settlers built their homes here to have a natural heat during the winter months. It gets very cold here during those times. The water is also pure and filled with Faerie's magic, so it is most coveted. Whoever controls the springs, controls a great power source. This is the reason why Michael chose to build a home here," he explains, looking around and taking it all in.

The one thing Michael is not, is stupid. He saw the long game and planned for it. While he knew I was coming because of that damn prophecy, I know nothing. It's frustrating, always playing catch-up.

"We need to move. There's going to be the shift change in five minutes, and I don't want them to hear us speaking," Shax says, ushering us along down the tunnel.

Cass lights his glow ball so that we can all see better, and my mind drifts to what this actually means. I'm going to save Noli and try not to get killed in the process. Surrounded by the people I trust the most, we are going to get her back. We have to; failure is not an option.

Shax, Cass, and Gunn lead our party with me sandwiched in the middle of Ash and Red in the rear. I know they are forming a protective circle around me, and I don't know whether to be irritated or to accept this for what it is —love.

"What's the plan when we get there, General?" I ask. He

chuckles at his new nickname and pokes me in the back. I turn around and offer him my best glare.

"Smart-ass," he says. "When we get to the cavern at the end of the tunnel system, there should be a door or latch opening up into the dungeon. We will go up in pairs and try to search as many of the cells as possible. We need to be quick and not cause a stir. The only variable I can see for this all to go wrong is if there are prisoners in the cells, and they alert the guards. The way Daniel described the layout, it seems that we will come up in the south hallway and have to turn right at the junction to find her. Let's hope he didn't set us up."

Thinking about all the ways this could go wrong, I send up a prayer to whoever is listening. I'm hoping the universe is on our side.

When we reach the cavern, there are stairs built into the wall climbing up to a singular door. It's so narrow, that one person can barely make it up without falling over. We trek slowly up, making sure our footing is safe and moving as quietly as possible. The door is solid wood with intricate symbols etched into it. Cass takes the lead and I follow behind him in anticipation of this happening. He reaches out a hand, and I place my hand over his. The door disengages, and the smell hits us. Rot and decay infiltrate my nose. I clasp my hand over my mouth and try not to throw up. It's so horrible, that it is obvious that terrible things happen here. I hope we aren't too late.

Filing into the hall, I take a look around. There are rows of sealed rooms with metal looking doors opening to each one. The floor is solid stone, but there are wet stains all over, and it reeks of waste. Rats, or the Fae equivalent, run across our feet looking for their next meal. I peek into the first door we see and wish I hadn't. There's a Fae strung up from the ceiling with his arms outstretched in a "V" shape. He's half-naked and filthy, with blood dripping down his chest from huge open gashes. It looks like someone cut him open and left him to bleed out.

I grip the handle of the door and try to pull it open. All I can think about is helping to save this man, but it won't budge. Tears form in my eyes, and I growl in frustration.

Red leans into me and whispers in my ear, "Azra, he's already dead. See that his energy is no longer there." I really look this time, and he is right — the Fae is gone.

I close my eyes and let out a silent scream of agony. The cruelty will end. Michael will feel every second of his death. I project to the prisoner, that I will see justice for him. I continue walking without looking into any more cells. I know if I do, we'll never find Noli. Coming to the junction, I turn right and march down the hall. This one isn't so quiet. Moans and screams echo off the walls, and I can't help but hold my hands up to my ears. It's torture hearing the pain and suffering that these Fae have to endure.

There's a scuffle ahead, and an arm grabs me by the waist and pushes me against the wall. *Be quiet. We need to wait for them to leave*, Red says. The minutes feel like hours as finally two Fae guards in the colors of the Light walk down the hallway. They turn down where we are, and before either of them can engage, Shax and Cass have them dead on the floor. I didn't even see them move. They hide in the shadows so completely that the guards never had a chance.

Red pushes me forward, and we continue on. I'm still in shock but find my strength in knowing we'll be getting Noli out of here today. Shax and Cass take the lead, daggers in their hands, ready to fight should we have to. Gunn and Ash are behind us with their own weapons, protecting my back.

Voices can be heard at the end of the hallway where there is a low glow of light. My anticipation picks up, and I feel my magic respond. It's ready to protect and defend her mates and soul-bonded. I want so badly to just blow up this whole damn mountain, but there could be innocent people here.

Cass and Shax pick up their pace, and I scrunch my eyebrows in confusion because this wasn't part of the plan. What are they doing? Before I can say anything, they round the corner out of sight. Red pushes me along to the final door and tries to get it open. I'm torn worrying about the guys and opening the door. The magic symbols are on this door also, except Cass isn't here to help.

"You're going to have to open it yourself," Ash says from behind me. Her voice sounds on edge. She's itching for a fight as well.

I place my hands on the handle and push just enough magic into it so that the door handle lights up with it. A click sounds, and the door pushes open. Gunn pulls me to him, and Red and Ash pile into the room while I wait. I try to struggle out of his grip. I need to see her. Make sure she's alive, and let her know I'm here.

Red comes rushing out of the room with Noli draped in his arms, and my heart immediately sinks into my stomach. She isn't conscious. I can't see if she is breathing. Red is hurrying down the way we came and isn't stopping so I can check her out. I'm running full out trying to catch up with them. Realizing Shax and Cass are still not with us, I look back to see where they are.

"Keep going. They will catch up," Gunn says. He takes my upper arm and pushes me forward. I'm so torn at this moment. Two parts of my life are in different directions. My power tries to reach out. I can't help it; I'm scared. I don't know the answers to what's happening, and it's all so fast.

Gunn pulls me closer and kisses my mouth with a consuming kiss. I'm so shocked by this that my power ebbs back to manageable.

"No bombs, Azra," he says with lust in his eyes. He's having a hard time keeping it together too. My assassin is nervous for his mates. Footsteps running down the hall break me out of the bubble. Cass and Shax come running down with soldiers on their heels. This spurs me on, and I make my way for the door that Red and Ash have escaped through. We all reach it together and quickly move down the stairs. I hear grunting and grinding behind me and know one of the guys is trying to get the door closed. Carefully turning on the steps, I put out a blast of my magic towards the door, and it shuts with a thud. Three sets of wide eyes look at me while I shrug and continue down the death-trap stairs.

We make it outside in record time. Red is still carrying an unconscious Noli. "Please tell me she's alive," I yell at his back. We aren't stopping, and I need to know.

"She's breathing, but let's get back to Jezebel so we can get the fuck out of here before the whole guard finds us," he says. This urges me on further, and I pick up the pace, letting my magic fuel my legs to help me run faster. The outlet feels amazing, and I can't believe how fast I am. I quickly catch up to Ash, who looks over at me with pride in her face. My Arion chose well for a mate.

Jezebel is exactly where we left her. Gunn takes Noli from Red as they shift back into Arion form. We each climb up on our mounts and take off into the trees like thunderclap clouds, so fast that you can hardly see us running. The world is a blur, and I'm starting to feel a bit nauseous. Grey is holding on with a death grip. To my left is Jezebel and Gunn holding Noli. Jezebel is glowing pure white as she is keeping up with us. I see her silhouette, and I can see a long horn on her head. My shock is all over my face and leaks through the bond. Five voices laugh in my head while I put two and two together and realize that Jezebel is a fucking unicorn.

18

THE BALL

*T*he castle is alive with activity when we finally make it back. There are Fae running around all over, and a buzz is in the air. Getting back was a harder journey. We had to take a different direction to ensure that we weren't followed. This tacked on an additional day of travel.

Noli is still unconscious. My insides feel like they have been liquified every time I stare at her face. If she wasn't breathing, I would think she was dead. I'm starting to worry, but Red says the healers at the palace will help. He and Ash have taken her to the medical ward. I was nervous leaving her, but I'm no use to anyone in this condition.

"What's going on?" I ask Shax as he jumps down off of Ash. He looks around and stops a server passing us with different types of fabrics draped over his arms.

"Henry, what's going on?" he asks. The Fae stops and bows to us all before answering.

"Your Highnesses, Changer, tomorrow is the Summer Ball. We've been preparing for it since you left," he says. He's looking around at us, and I can tell he needs to be somewhere.

"Thank you, Henry. Please, carry on," Shax says, dismissing the Fae. He looks over at me, and I see the regret in his face. He's going to tell me something I do not like.

"Why are you looking at me like that? You do realize we can't go to a ball. We have a revolution to run," I say with a smirk.

"Azra, we have to go. It's not something my mother will be okay with us skipping," Shax says, trying to comfort me. I really don't want to get dressed up in front of another Fae court.

"She's going to announce my allegiance to the Dark, isn't she?" I ask. This is fucking terrifying, and I don't know how I'm going to get out of it.

"Probably, but we can work around it," Cass says. They both look confident that this is going to work out.

"I don't like it," Grey says. He's skeptical as usual. "There's too much of a possibility for this to blow up in our faces. How is she going to get out of publicly declaring her allegiance? Does the Queen do the same ritual that Michael does to make pacts binding?"

"Yes, but I have something that might work to counter it," Shax says.

"Might work? Listen, *Cat.* we need more than just might," Grey responds. He's right. Not having a guarantee when it comes to the Queen could mean that we're stuck here working for her.

"How about we table this for now? Let's go in and get rested. I need to check on Noli in a bit, but first, eat and then sleep," I say, walking toward the front doors. Entering the foyer, I can see the Queen has spared no expense on decorations. The black marble acts as the backdrop to the incredible silks that hang from the ceiling. The floor is so polished, it looks like one slab of onyx. Looking down, I can see my reflection, tired and dirty.

There are accents of silver highlighting the darker corners. Chaise lounges and groups of comfortable chairs are in different sections, giving it a lounge vibe. Beautiful flower arrangements are dispersed around the room to balance out the masculinity of the marble. It's all very beautiful and luxurious.

"Let's get upstairs before someone stops us," Shax says. "I have a feeling that this is going to be bigger than we originally thought." My look says it all. I'd rather be running from the Light guard again.

Making our way up to our suite, I find that not only is the foyer decorated, but so is the whole palace. The sexy vibe of the silks are running up the stairs, and the vases that are normally tucked into the corners, are now a mirror image of the ones downstairs.

When we approach our door, I can hear a commotion coming from our rooms. Gunn reaches out his hand and holds me in place. He places his finger over his lips in a 'be quiet' signal. I nod my head and pull out the Changer sword from its scabbard. The guys get their own weapons ready. Cass moves to the door and stretches his hand to open it, but he keeps his body to the side to keep it from the exposed doorway. Shax takes the opposite side, and Grey and Gunn flank me to the left.

Pushing the unlocked door open, we pile in the room ready to defend ourselves only to find Miniel and Sophie standing arguing with a few of the servants about the quality of light in the room. Apparently, the huge drapes are a problem for seeing their vision.

I stop in my tracks totally stunned. The last time I saw

them was the night of the Light court dinner. I didn't think I'd see them ever again.

"What are you guys doing here?" I ask. My voice shows astonishment for how this could be real.

"We escaped when Michael opened the portal to let the army in," Sophie says. She's still just as beautiful as the last time I saw her. Purple hair cascading down her back with pointed ears showing just a bit. She has on her usual black outfit— leather pants with a vest so tight that her boobs look squished. She's otherworldly. She looks so much stronger and more vibrant. Faerie must be returning her true powers.

"I can't believe you guys got out! How did you convince the Queen to allow you to stay?" I wonder out loud. It must have not been easy since they were a part of the Light court.

"That was easy. We were part of Her Majesty's court before we got kidnapped to the Light. She welcomed us back— well, as much as she can be welcoming," Miniel says matter-of-factly.

"That seems a bit convenient to me," Grey says. Ever the skeptic.

"He's right. How do we know we can trust you?" Gunn says. He must not know them from before.

"Guys, they aren't here to trade secrets. They're here to help us get ready," I say. Turning toward Miniel I ask, "Is there time for a quick nap before we start this process?" There might just be a touch of excitement in my voice.

"Afraid not, Azra. You all are due down in the ballroom in three hours. I still have to fit everyone and make alterations. It's going to be tight as it is," Miniel replies.

"If that's the case, I'm going to go check in on Logan before we get this primping process under way. I need to make sure he's doing okay with Anna," Grey says, exiting back out of the room. I think he just doesn't want to get dressed up.

"We also need to do makeup. The rest of the guys can get fitted first, and I'll do your face in the meantime. Greyson can get fitted when he comes back," Sophie says.

Rolling my eyes so far in the back of my head, I stamp my feet like a toddler and walk into my bathroom. I hear a chorus of laughter behind me. This is going to be a long night.

Three hours later we are dressed to kill and walking down the stairs to the party. Music is filtering through the halls. I can hear a violin and maybe a cello? It's beautiful and depressing—just like this court.

Approaching the doors, there's a line of Fae waiting to be announced. The crowd parts and lets us through. There are hushed whispers as we walk toward the door, and I know that all eyes are trained on us.

"Why is it important to have people announce you into the party? I never got that," I ask my princes. They are delicious in their three-piece suits and matching ties. Miniel matched the guys to my dress. I'm wearing a hunter-green silk gown. The bodice is low cut in the front, almost to my belly button, and is being held up by two thin straps. The skirt flares out into a wave of green silk trailing down to the floor. My back is exposed, and while I am a little cold, the dress is so simple and beautiful that I don't mind.

"It shows status. The Fae love for people to know where they are located in the hierarchy. The closer to the Queen, the more respected they are, or so they hope. It really is all just for show," Cass explains. He looks down at me with a smile, and my heart stops for a second. He's so beautiful.

"Can I have the pleasure of walking you in?" Shax asks, placing my arm in his. I give him a sexy grin and nod my head in agreement. His hair is nicely combed to the side, but a little rogue curl peaks out at the nape of his neck. I want nothing more than to run my hands through it while I feel him move beneath me.

A throat clears behind us, and I turn around to see Gunn adjusting his pants. "You may want to turn down the mind projecting, Az. We can feel and see what you want Shax to do later."

"Let's get this shit show over with. I don't want to be down here one more minute than necessary," Grey says from beside Gunn. He's just as stunning in his jacket. He's so on edge about this evening that he insisted his wings be out. Miniel had to cut out places in his jacket for them to be on display.

"His Royal Highnesses, Prince Shax of the Dark and Cassiel of the Light. The Changer Azrael, and her harem," the guard announces. Trumpets blare, and the doors open before us. I slide my other arm into Cass's to make sure I don't trip in these four-inch heels Miniel insisted on.

Walking down the stairs with both princes on my arms, the whole crowd turns toward me. I see the eyes of Fae that I have never seen before dissecting me, wanting me to be something that I'm not, something I will never be. They want me to be the thing that I fear most. Someone who won't stand up for what they believe in, but who will conform because it is easier.

My legs wobble a bit under their scrutiny, but my guys are right there to hold me up. They're always there when I need them the most. Even though Gunn is new to our band of misfits, I know he's just as connected to us as the others. He's ready to defend and protect us. I send a pulse of gratitude through the bond to my men and pick my up head up a little higher. I want to show these Fae that I'm not going to be their puppet. I'm a strong Fae, one that will take on the biggest of the bads and come out on top.

The ballroom is set up as you would imagine the Dark Court to be. There are long tables surrounding the room, and the same black silks that are on the ceilings in the foyer are draped throughout this room as well. The tables are covered in crystal cloths, and accents of the silver flowers are everywhere. A dais is at the back of the room. It's raised above all so the Queen can see all the activity. A page leads us over towards the dais, and we file into our chairs, Gunn holding out mine. Shax is seated on the right of the Queen's chair, and to the left of it is Daniel who waves with a smirk. A man I have never seen before is seated next to him.

"Zagan," Shax says, with a growl as he takes his seat. The tension in the air picks up, and my eyes go wide. The hate is apparent between these two. The man nods his head at Shax and turns his eyes back to the door, thoroughly ignoring us.

"Who is that?" I whisper to Shax as soon as we are all seated.

"My mother's familiar. He's a nasty creature. He can take on any animal form he wishes, including human, and is quite sneaky about it. He was the other jaguar in the throne room when you first arrived. He wreaks havoc wherever he goes and is the essence of my mother's power. He's her spy and confidante. Stay away from him," he warns. I glance very quickly over to this Zagan and notice that he's staring at me. I have never felt the caress of such darkness before. He's just as ugly and corrupt as the Queen.

A loud bang sounds, and everyone's attention goes toward the doors. The guards announce the Queen, and she glides in with a flourish. If I thought my dress was stunning, it's nothing compared to hers. She looks otherworldly.

The dress is done in shades of black and gray. It matches the décor, as I thought it would, but it makes the whole thing come together. The top is off the shoulders and low cut. You can see the swell of her breasts, and her creamy skin contrasts with the darkness of the material. It's form fitting to the waist and the skirts bellow out in waterfalls of fabric. It's so thin and wispy it looks like she is made out of spun sugar. The tips of the dress brush the hall floor and are a light gray, the color of clouds. The dress is a masterpiece. Sparkling diamonds accent it all over, so when she moves the light bounces off it, giving it the effect that she is twinkling.

"You can close your mouth," Grey says, tapping my shoulder. I don't know how he convinced Cass to sit in the third chair. It fits him, though, being my second guy. His power is so much stronger than I originally thought. His white wings are on display for all to see. They are ruffled, and you can tell he is irritated, but he's gorgeous, nonetheless.

"Sorry. She's just so stunning," I say, closing my mouth and turning to the guys. Their masks are back on, showing no emotion. I can feel Gunn is uneasy as she walks toward the dais. He hates her.

We all rise and wait for her to make her way up. Zagan met her at the stairs and helps her to her chair. Everyone bows down as she walks over, and I curtsy, but never lower my head. She isn't my Queen.

"Changer, ever the pretty little thing," she sneers, giving me the once over.

"Your Majesty, you look breathtaking," I say honestly. I think the only thing we can both agree on is how beautiful she is.

"I know," she says, taking a seat. The room quickly follows as all attention is still on the Queen. There's dead silence that is starting to feel uncomfortable. She breaks it with her usual charisma.

"Welcome, my subjects. I have invited you all here to witness the return of the Changer," she says. The crowd cheers, stomping their feet and clapping so loud, I think I might go deaf.

Raising her hand, she continues, "Tonight she will declare her loyalty to the Dark. Since Michael has brought the fight to us, we will answer in blood and death. He thinks we are to fear him. Well, I say bring it! Let's show him how the Dark does not forget, and how we have grown in strength since the last battle," she says, raising her glass to the ceiling. "For the Dark! For Blood! For Death!"

The hall erupts into a storm of shouts, whistles, and clapping. They're riled up, and the energy is suffocating. I can feel their intentions, and none are about liberation. It is all about revenge.

Grey grabs my hand underneath the table and sends some reassurance down the bond. He must have felt how nervous I am. I look at both princes and see that they are used to this type of posturing. They are true to themselves with a stoic mask looking onto the crowd. Gunn is still, with waves of anger rolling off of him. I turn to see Daniel cheering with the rest of them, and the Queen looking at him like they got very well acquainted while we were gone. It doesn't surprise me one bit; Daniel is an opportunist.

The meal passes by with tension and discomfort. I'm only able to manage to eat some soup, and a bit of meat.

My stomach is rolling with all of the evil in the air. When the last course is cleared, the Fae below us get up, and the tables magically vanish into thin air. A large band comes through a side door, and they begin to play what I can only assume is the dancing music for this portion of the ball. One by one, the Fae all approach the dais and bow down to the Queen, offering gifts and words of solidarity. They worship her, and I feel her glee as they grovel and say nice things to her. My revulsion is taken to another level. I don't know how much longer I'm going to be able to sit here.

"Azra, may I have the pleasure of a dance?" A voice says from behind me. I turn in my chair and see Daniel with his hand outstretched. Grey's wings flutter in annoyance, and I hear the Queen snicker.

Shax kicks me under the chair, and I plaster a smile on my face. "Of course," I say, rising and taking his hand in mine. He leads me down onto the dance floor. Fae of all types are dancing around in circles to a song I have never heard. I was never a good dancer, especially ballroom, so I allow Daniel to lead me around the room. His movements are graceful and honed, that of a prince. It doesn't take him long to get to the point.

"I see you saved the witch," he states, with one of his cocky smiles.

"I don't know why you keep calling her that. She isn't a witch," I reply.

"I thought she was your best friend," he states, tilting his head in a confused expression.

"She is, and she isn't a witch," I say, hearing the doubt in my own voice. I've known Noli for two years, and I have never seen her use any powers. I mean the tarot stuff is just for fun, right?

"That's hilarious," he says, laughing into my ear. He's too close, and I'm starting to get annoyed.

"Did you need something, Daniel?" I ask, putting some space between us.

"I just wanted a chance to dance with the gorgeous Changer. Soon you will be covered in so much blood that I might never get another chance," he leers. The sinister smile he has on his face makes a chill run through me. A pang of fear hits me, and before I know it, hands are snatching me away from him. A feeling of calmness and security smacks into me. Cass is here.

"I'll take it from here, brother," he says, pulling me into the crowd of dancers. He doesn't even give Daniel an opportunity to reply. I look over and see the jealousy in Daniel's eyes. Whether it is for me, or Cass, I don't know.

"Thank you for saving me," I say, leaning into him. His calming scent of winter and storms makes me relax a bit more.

"I will always save you," he says, placing a kiss on my head and holding me close. We dance like this for the rest of the song, and then each of my guys cut in, switching off songs and fending off Fae who try to get too close to me. Having them all around me, dancing and laughing, actually makes me forget all about the bad this evening represents.

Midnight strikes, and the hall goes quiet. The Queen steps down from the dais for the first time and takes center stage on the dance floor. Zagan and Daniel flank her, and it becomes apparent to me the real reason why he chose to come to court. Revenge might have been the motivation at first, but he's here for power. He's seeking out the winner. He couldn't be any more wrong.

"It is time! Azra, join me here to take your vow," she says.

Her voice booms throughout the hall. My stomach drops, and I look over to Shax. Didn't he have a plan?

Guys now would be a good time to fill me in with what the fuck to do. I shout at them through the bond. None of them move. They create a wall of no emotion behind me as I walk toward the Queen.

Approaching her feels like I am walking to my death. She's everything I don't want to be. Michael is cruel and absolute, but he's true to who he is. There is no doubt that he's truly evil. Lucifer, she's something else. She is saccharine sweet with a poison center. You don't realize you're fucked until it's too late.

As I approach, she reaches out her hand for mine. I don't know why I would need to place it there, so I look at her with a question. She huffs in annoyance and pulls out a dagger from the folds of her skirt. I jump back in hesitation.

"I'm not going to stab you. We need to make a blood oath, and I need your blood to do it. I'm sure you are familiar with blood bonds by now," she says, taunting me. I guess she really does know about Red.

"What is this bond for?" I ask, my voice is a bit shakier than I would like. I don't want to show my fear, but it's hard with her. She's so intimidating.

"In order for your Changer gifts to work for the Dark, you need to swear a blood bond to me. It's like an insurance policy, in case you want to jump ship and join the other side," she explains. The smile that covers her face is purely for show. Her energy is pumping out anger that I'm questioning her, and anticipation to get this done, because this blood bond is something different. I'm walking into a trap.

Daniel fidgets behind her, and I give him my attention for a split second. I don't even see her move. Her hand grabs mine so hard that it turns moon white, and my Changer powers start to glow. Instinct has taken over, and my oil-slick wings pop out. If she doesn't stop touching me, I'm going to blow this whole chamber to pieces. She raises the knife, and in slow motion, I watch as it plunges down toward my exposed forearm. My fire lights up the room, and she drops her hand from my wrist. Grabbing hers to her chest.

"You little bitch! Using hellfire is punishable by death!" she screams. Shax runs up behind us and puts his body in front of mine. All the men tense up, and I can see Zagan sizing them up if something should go down. Gunn is dripping with glee. He wants this fight. He's waited for it for so long.

"Mother, you surprised her. Azra doesn't know how to fully control her powers yet. When she's scared or angry, they just react. Please let me help," he begs. The submission in his voice makes me want to scream out. No one should make my alpha feel like this!

Before she can answer there is a terrible crash, and the windows of the hall blow out. The night air rushes in, and the ground begins to shake. My first thought is it must be a dragon, but when I turn to see the cause; a gasp is caught on my lips. Noli. She's awake and she's fucking pissed. Her hair is moving around her with a current that isn't visible anywhere. Her dress is torn, and dirty, but her eyes are glowing a pure white. She is orchestrating the power surge throughout the room. A storm picks up, and I have two seconds to grab for Shax before we are picked up and thrown out of one of the windows.

Landing with a thud on the hard-packed dirt, I pick myself up and look around for the others. We are all clustered together, and I thank whoever is listening for that.

Standing up, I unclasp the skirts of my dress and reveal the pants I have been wearing underneath the whole time. I break the heels off of my shoes and take off running to where I can feel my Arion starting trouble. The guys are right on my heels, but I don't wait for them. When I get to the commotion, I see it's not just Red, but an army of Fae I don't recognize. They aren't in the Light's uniform. They just look like a very powerful group of Fae, clustered together for one purpose. Our purpose. I race over to Red who moves just at the right time so that I can settle myself on his back. Grey takes into the skies, and Shax and Cass saddle up on Ash. Gunn is the last to find his mount, but he doesn't have to take long, because Noli rides up on Jezebel soon after.

Looking back toward the castle, I see the Dark trying to get control of this new army, but they don't have a chance. The Fae who have come to aid me are too powerful. The Queen is front and center but can only concentrate on burning one Fae at a time. It seems like her powers aren't as vast as I thought. There's a witch with pink hair standing proud in front of three jaguars, similar to Shax's cat. Her hands are outstretched, and a wall of Earth is erected between the Dark and this mystery group of Fae. I lean into Red, and he doesn't need any more encouragement.

We have escaped the Dark. We are free. We are in so much shit.

he End...for now.

ACKNOWLEDGMENTS

There are so many people to thank. This book was harder to write than Death Card. So many people enjoyed the first book, I didn't think I'd be able to measure up with the second. I struggled with Azra and her mates, but I think all the months it took me to write it were worth it. I hope you truly enjoyed it.

The first people I want to thank is you, dear reader. Without you, I wouldn't have a career as an author. Thank you for taking a chance on me and reading all the words I write. You all have been a blessing to me, and I vow to keep writing to the best of my ability for you.

The Three other Pages - without you guys I would never be able to write the way I do. You all are so important to me, and there really isn't a day that goes by where I don't thank God, I found you. C.M. you're the writer I want to be when I group up. Your words infect so much emotion, and I feel your PASSION in each one. Your friendship lifts me up and gives me hope that we will one day get our retreat. Isobelle, without your constant guidance and cheerleading I would have given up long ago. Thank you for letting me know a little PAIN will get you the treasure you seek. Aspen, I wouldn't want another human being fighting in my corner. Your strength and dedication are immeasurable. Thanks for always going to WAR for me. I love you all.

Sosha, my GODDESS, you're truly the best PA an author could ask for. Your dedication and organization keep me sane. Your guidance has made me a better author. I wouldn't be where I am without you. I love you.

Nichol, thank you for all your help these last months. Your kickass skills with my website and graphics have really turned my brand into something special. I am truly grateful our paths merged. Love you girl!

Kala, thank you for all you've done. All the late-night chats, and words of encouragement. You truly are more than my editor, you're one of my dearest friends. I can't wait to see what the future brings us.

Nichole Witholder, another stunning cover. Thank you for taking my jumbled descriptions and turning it into a magnificent masterpiece.

To my beta team Thaís, Rachel, and Julie thank you for taking the time out of your days to help me make this book into an amazing tale. I'm so grateful for everything you have done. Without your knowledge and keen eyes, Claiming Death wouldn't be the awesome book it is.

Kristi, my soul sister, as the months go by, I know the one constant in my life is you. You keep me sane when I lose it and ground me when I have my head in the clouds. Thank you for always believing in me. I love you.

Momma, Ti amo più dell'aria che respiro. Grazie per avermi dato questa vita meravigliosa.

Lastly, thank you to my husband and two beautiful girls. There is no life without you in it. You are my everything, the reason I live and breathe. I love you.

AUTHOR'S NOTE

If you enjoyed Claiming Death, check out my other titles:

Death Card – The Changer Series – Book 1 https://www.
books2read.com/deathcard

Sinner's Harem – A Sinners and Saints Prequel Novella
https://www.books2read.com/sinnersharem

**If you'd like to stalk me here is where you can find me. I'd
love for you all to join the debauchery in the Wild Card!**

Wild Card Readers Group: https://www.facebook.com/
groups/acwildsreaders/

Facebook author page:
https://www.facebook.com/acwildsauthor/

Instagram: https://www.instagram.com/acwilds_author/

Twitter: https://twitter.com/ac_wilds

BookBub: https://www.bookbub.com/profile/a-c-wilds

Goodreads:
https://www.goodreads.com/author/show/18784983.A_C_Wilds

Website: https://www.acwilds.com

SNEAK PEEK AT SINNER'S HAREM - SAINTS AND SINNERS PREQUEL

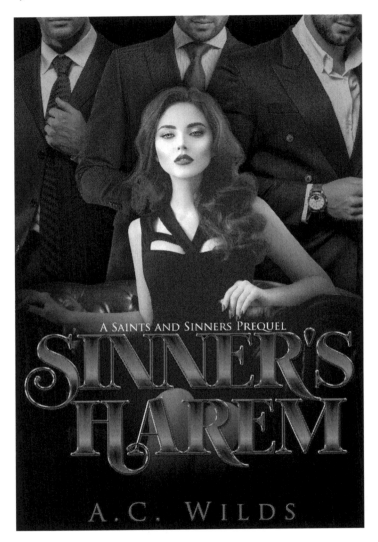

A SAINTS AND SINNERS PREQUEL

SINNER'S HAREM

A.C. WILDS

CHAPTER ONE

$\mathcal{T}$he sounds of people and honking horns bombard my senses. I am already on edge and nervous as hell. I've been in this city for three years, and I will never get over the vast number of people here. The subways are crowded, the buses are worse, and the streets are a jungle. You can't even walk a few feet without having to avoid a collision.

Work in this town is also few and far between for a woman like me. I have no skills to really put on a resume, and I never went to a traditional higher education school. The only way I could find any job was through a temp agency. Getting the jobs nobody wants and this one is no exception.

The new job that the temp agency sent me to is in the Financial District in lower Manhattan. It's one of the busiest places in the city during the day. People are milling around trying to get to work and all I can think about is, will I get lost again? As I glance down at my phone and verify the address, I am getting bumped all over and finally decide to move to the edge of the sidewalk. Looking up at the formidable building in front of me, I sigh heavily. It looks like something out of a movie. It must have a hundred floors.

It's a few days before Christmas, and this job just happened to pop up. No one wanted to take it because of the holiday, but I'm broke and need to pay rent. It gets cold in New York and heating is expensive. Food is also something I like to have around, so whatever jobs pop up I take. Walking through the huge glass doors, I approach the security desk.

"Good Morning, I am the new executive assistant temp for Bowman, Stanford, and Reynolds," I tell the woman, sitting behind the desk.

"ID please," she asks as she holds out her hand to me. I guess they aren't that friendly here. I dig in my bag and hand her my ID.

"Sign here," she says as she swings a tablet in my direction. I sign, and she hands me a temporary pass that gives me access to the building and the offices for the next three days.

"Take the elevator to the penthouse and ask the main secretary for further instructions," she explains and then dismisses me by looking down at her paperwork again.

I walk over to the half a dozen elevators along the far wall and press the up button. There are a bunch of people waiting with me, but none of them seem to be speaking to each other. They are all looking at their phones or tablets: the elevator dings and the doors in front of me open. As I step in, people pile in while I press the button for the penthouse. We stop on multiple floors, and before I know it I am the last one in the lift. The elevator comes to a stop with a little bounce, and the doors open up.

Walking out, I approach the reception desk. "Hi, my

name is Tamara Sinner. I am the new executive admin temp." I tell the man behind the counter with a big smile.

He looks me over and nods his head. Turning around he grabs a tablet and gives it to me. "Here you go. Your office is the last one on the left," he says with a sly smile... like he knows something I don't.

"Thanks," I tell him, reaching out to grab the tablet and make my way down the hall. It smells like paper, glue, and peppermint. It's not unpleasant, but it isn't welcoming either. All of the offices have glass walls, and I glance around at the people on phones or typing away on their computers. I notice that they are all men, and I don't see another woman anywhere.

At the end of the hall are two huge oak doors with brass handles. The walls that are connected to the doors are solid. The doors are both impressive and foreboding. My office is directly to the side of the entrance. Walking into the room and around the desk, I notice there is only a single stack of papers with a note on top.

'When you get in, come into my office,' it reads. Signed with just a last name, Bowman.

Taking off my jacket, I hang it on the coat hanger in the corner and place my bag inside the table right below it. As I walk around the desk, I look at the stack and see that everything is written in some code that I have no idea how to decipher. With a sigh, I walk out of my office.

I knock on the impressive doors, but no one answers. I try again using a little more force. Nothing. I turn the knob, and it opens easily for me. The door is heavy, but I manage to push it open. "Hello?" I call out into a vast lounge type room. There are couches directly in front of me perpendicular to a huge gas fireplace. The place is done in grays and blacks with a lot of marble accents throughout. There is massive floor to ceiling windows looking out on the Manhattan skyline. You can even see the Statue of Liberty in the distance. It's such a beautiful view.

As I am gazing out the window, a door opens in the corner of the room. Out steps a man dressed in a black custom designer suit with shiny dress shoes. He stands around 5'6" and is broad in his chest. His curly dark hair is messily tossed all over, which is an extreme contrast to his body-hugging suit.

He stops when he sees me. "Can I help you?" he asks, giving me an appraising look. His too blue eyes bore into me, and I feel heat rush up from my toes to my face. I must be red as a tomato.

"I'm Tamara Sinner, the new temp," I squeak out. Looking at him, I see that he is impossibly beautiful, and I know that it is going to make the next three days very hard to concentrate.

"Sinner? That's your last name?" he chuckles at me.

"Yes, it is. My German ancestors had their name changed into English when they came over to Ellis Island in the late 1800s. It was originally Sunder which translates into sinner in English." I explain to him. This man is making me so nervous my fingers are twisted at my side. I'm sweating all over, and I feel a bit light headed.

"Interesting. Ok Sinner, let me get my partners, and we can begin discussing what it is we need from you for the next three days," he tells me with a bright smile. He turns and walks through the door he previously came out of.

CHAPTER TWO

While he is gone, I take it upon myself to pour some water from the bar on the far side of the room. The cold liquid is laced with cucumber and lemon and tastes fantastic sliding down my very parched throat.

I sit on one of the couches and wait for my bosses to return. Looking around I notice different decorations throughout, and see there are subtle touches of Christmas all around. A tree in the corner done in white lights with simple red and green ball ornaments. A bough of pine is hung over the fireplace, and a wreath is on the door the hot guy walked through. It is all very pretty but looks very staged and impersonal. There is no character in here.

After waiting for twenty minutes they finally walk through the door. I rise from the couch as they approach. Holy cannoli! If I thought the first guy was attractive, these other two are even more so. The man on the right is dressed in a chocolate brown suit with an ivory colored button down shirt. His tie is burnt orange color. This definitely is a man who isn't afraid to express himself. He has short black hair, and I can see a tattoo peeking out of the collar of his shirt. I am so intrigued and enthralled at the same time. The third man is smaller than the other two, but makes up for it in broadness. He is built like a linebacker. His suit is a traditional navy blue with a cornflower blue shirt and matching tie. His hair is blond and styled into a neat side part. Looking further, I notice his hands are the size of dinner plates. He licks his lips when I meet his gaze, and I have to rub my thighs together to release some of the tension instantly building inside of me.

"Sinner this is Rhys Stanford and Roman Reynolds, and I am Ryder Bowman. You will be working directly for us over the next few days. We have particular tasks that need to be completed before Christmas, and our regular executive admin was just fired for stealing money. Hence the reason why we needed to bring someone in right away." Bowman explains.

"Can I ask what those tasks are? I saw a stack of papers on the desk, but I have never seen writing like that before." I ask him.

"You have got to be kidding me, Ryder! I thought you cleared this with the temp agency. We need someone who is able to translate our analytics into the system. This is not going to work!" Rhys yells. He looks pissed off, but the smaller one, Roman, looks amused. If his grin is anything to go by.

"Relax Rhys; I am sure Ms. Sinner here is quite capable of learning a few new things. Besides, the analytics can wait until the new year to be completed." Roman says with a bit of depth to his voice. A voice that I could get lost in.

I swallow the rest of the water in my glass before I can even think about what I am doing. Instantly I regret it when

Ryder's eyes begin to widen with anticipation. My insides heat up, and I definitely feel a draw to this man.

"Fine, but after the three days, she is gone," Rhys says and storms off into the next room.

"Sorry about that, he can get a little bit volatile sometimes. He has certain...requirements and if they aren't met, he gets a bit cranky." Roman explains to me.

"I understand. Could you maybe enlighten me on what else I am to do while I am here?" I ask him looking into his eyes. We stare at each other for a few seconds as the tension in the room builds. I am starting to feel very small amongst these powerful men.

"The usual, answer calls, manage our calendars, and accompany us to meetings to take minutes. We sometimes forget to take breaks and relax, so that is something you will have to remind us to do as well . We usually work through lunch, so ordering out will be your job as well." Ryder explains.

"Sounds good to me, where would you like me to start?" I ask them both, looking from one to the other. They are both so beautiful; it is hard to choose which one I'd want in my bed. What! Where did that come from? Focus Sinner.

"You can start in the boardroom. I have a bunch of papers that need to be filed, and it will be good for you to get acquainted with our files. We have a meeting in about ten minutes and would like you to sit in on it." Roman says as he walks toward the door.

I follow behind both of them through the door with the wreath. Immediately, the atmosphere changes. This room is a bit darker than the others with only sconces on the walls, lighting up the room in an eerie glow. This isn't a typical meeting space. Four doors are connecting to this room. One is slightly ajar, and I can see a sink and mirror. That must be their bathroom. The other entries are shut tightly. Maybe their private offices?

I walk all the way into the room and up to the impressive boardroom table in the center. Rubbing my hand across the shiny varnish, I see that it is a deep maroon color carved from a massive tree. It had to have cost a fortune. Ten leather office chairs are surrounding it. Rhys and Ryder take a seat near the head of the table, while Roman stands near me.

"This is our meeting area. We like to keep everything a bit more relaxed than a normal conference room. I can't stand fluorescent lights, so we switched to these scones to give it a warm feel in here." Roman explains to me.

"The table is gorgeous. I love the dark wood." I tell him, looking directly into his eyes again. I need to stop doing that, his stare is starting to do all kinds of things to my girly parts.

"I'm glad you like it. It is custom made and has a bunch of...extras that we can show you later," he says in a sultry voice. Oh my God, I am going to melt right here.

A knock sounds on the door, and I move to answer it. Before me stands a very beautiful woman in a trench coat. She has long red hair, emerald green eyes and is built like a model. "Hello, may I help you?" I ask her with a smile on my face.

"I'm here to see Roman, Rhys, and Ryder," she tells me with a smile all her own.

"Come in please," I say to her as I step to the side and allow her to enter the room.

"Hi boys," she says to the men standing at the table. "Miss me?" None of them say anything, but Rhys approaches her. He holds her upper arms on both sides and leans in to kiss her. Their kiss is full of passion and is sexy as all hell. I try to look away, but it is just impossible.

"Audra, this is Sinner," Roman says to her when they break the kiss.

I offer a little wave and say, "Hello."

"Hi darling," she says. Then she turns to Rhys and asks, "Will she be joining us."

He gets a very dark expression on his face. "Depends," he says to her while looking right at me. "She is a little new."

What the hell does that mean? I thought they wanted me to take minutes? Looking over at the other two partners in confusion, I see Ryder is removing his jacket and rolling up his sleeves. There are some very impressive tattoos all up and down his forearms. All done in a beautiful array of colors.

Roman removes his tie and places it gently on the table. I am starting to get a little worried why everyone is taking off articles of clothing and then it happens. Audra unbuckles her trench and lets it fall to the floor. She is wearing nothing but a bra and panties. Her stockings are held up by a garter belt, and her black patent leather red heels are at least five inches high.

I immediately divert my gaze and blush at the same time. What the fuck is going on? "Um... Mr. Bowman, I think I will wait in my office for your meeting to end. Just let me know when I should come back." I tell him holding my hand up to my face to shield my view of the gorgeous half-naked woman in the room.

"I would prefer you to stay and watch," Roman says to me.

Holy mother of fucking God. "Excuse me? Did you say you wanted me to watch you all have sex with this woman?" I ask him, clutching my chest in mock disgust. If I am honest, I am turned on as all fuck right now. I would love to watch; frankly I would like to participate, but I need this paycheck and can't take a chance losing it.

"That is what I said, yes," he says in a flat tone like he is talking about what to have for lunch.

"Gentleman, I don't think it is appropriate for me to be here. If I didn't need the money so badly, I would walk out these doors and not look back." I say with a fake shocked tone.

"You're lying" This comes out of Rhys's mouth which is currently pressed up against Audra's neck. "The moment we suggested it you crossed your legs and parted your lips. You want this as bad as we do."

I stare at him because how can I deny myself the truth? I don't act on it though. Instead, I turn on my heels and walk out of the boardroom.

Printed in Great
Britain
by Amazon